THE MAN WHO FELL TOO FAR

ROGER COREA

ISBN: 978-0-578-85333-8

RCC Publications

THE MAN WHO FELL TOO FAR

BY ROGER COREA · RELEASE DATE: January 29, 2021

In Corea's mid-1990s thriller, a series of violent crimes torments citizens in small-town New York.

While servicing a 40-foot utility pole, line-worker Jeff Walden falls from the bucket when his truck rolls. Medics rush him to the hospital, where his friend Michael Alexander, a financial adviser, anxiously awaits. The next day, Michael discovers that Jeff, in spite of his serious injuries, isn't in his hospital bed.

Shortly thereafter, an unknown assailant attacks a male-female couple and rapes the woman. The local police chief suggests the culprit is Jeff, whom Michael hasn't been able to locate.

Jeff is surrounded by brutal men in his life, from his brother Billy, who beat Jeff's wife, Francine, and got her hooked on cocaine, to Francine's father, who doesn't veil his animosity for his son-in-law. When a subsequent murder hits close to home, still -missing Jeff is once again a suspect. This time, some cops even eye Michael. Meanwhile, Jeff and Francine's 13-year-old son, who lives with foster parents, mysteriously vanishes. When a baddie ultimately guns for Michael and Jeff, more deaths are unavoidable.

Corea's uncompromising novel abounds with ferocious scenes and unsympathetic characters. Michael, for one, is a flawed protagonist who makes at least one very bad choice. Others, like Billy, are thoroughly loathsome. Characters endure bullying, domestic abuse, and worse. The author maintains a somber but engaging storyline with blunt metaphors: "Michael's skull was pounding as if someone had unloaded a pallet of concrete masonry bricks on his head."

Plenty of viable suspects keep the plot humming and unpredictable. It all culminates in a frenzied final act, and though someone unmasks the killer(s), the ending leaves quite a few things unresolved.

A hard-hitting, bleak murder mystery.

Pub Date: Jan. 29, 2021
ISBN: 978-0-57885333-8
Page Count: 212
Review Posted Online: Feb 4,2021
Review Program: KIRKUS
Categories: CRIME & LEGAL THRILLER | DETECTIVES & PRIVATE INVESTIGATORS | THRILLER | MYSTERY & DETECTIVE

READERS' TESTIMONIALS

We who live for the opportunity to devour a new book – as we might an exquisitely prepared favorite meal – this latest from Roger Corea is a page turner of the first order. Enjoy…or Bon Appetite!

Jack Benjamin

The Man Who Fell Too Far is a story of true friendships and intrigue. A real mystery that had me guessing until the end who done it! Roger Corea develops his characters in a way that makes you really care about them and want them to succeed. A real pleasurable and exciting read!

Robin Kukla

A psychological mystery thriller that tears a small town in the Adirondacks apart and delves into the deep-rooted secrets that bind them together. A lot of unexpected twists and turns that kept me riveted from beginning to end.

Lawrence Cilento

As with all Roger Corea's books, I was taken by his ability to paint a picture and have the reader enter that world, kind of like the rabbit hole in Alice In Wonderland. I thoroughly enjoyed his most recent undertaking.

Robert Tobin

Surprising twists and turns to this plot that takes place in Upstate New York, as well as some valuable insightful dialogue that could only be authored by an introspective intellect.

Susan Rice

The Man Who Fell Too Far is not only a psychological thriller that will keep you guessing until the very end, but a story about the emotional abuse of a child and his mother that will pull at your heart. A tangled web of destruction of a successful business man, the murder of the woman he loves, and his attempt to save his best friend from self-destruction are all wrapped up into one gripping thriller. Two men on a tense roller coaster ride of intrigue that keeps you on the edge of your seat wondering *who fell too far*.

Mary Jane Blum

I love thrillers! *The Man Who Fell Too Far* is one of the best! Half way through the novel I thought I had it all figured out. Boy, was I wrong. Usually, as an avid reader, I finish a novel in a month or so. This novel was different. I couldn't put it down and finished it in two days! I highly recommend this novel to anyone looking for an exciting reading experience!

Larry Wiese

Once in a while I come across a stimulating reading experience that I want to share with my friends and colleagues. *The Man Who Fell Too Far* is a thriller I would place in that category. The author's ability to portray the internal emotions of the characters was absolutely brilliant!

Rob O'Neil

This book is full of believable and interesting characters and all are connected by bizarre situations. It has been a while since I read a book that is hard to put down. I've already ordered another Roger Corea novel.

Mark Kukla

DEDICATION

For his loyalty, kindness, and concern for others, this book is dedicated to Jeff Williams who passed away January 16, 2020. He earned his "ticket" to heaven by the manner in which he lived his life.

Books by Roger Corea

www.rogercorea.com

Authors page at www.amazon.com

1. Scarback – This is so Much More to Fishing Than Catching Fish
2. The Duesenberg Caper
3. GTO – Race to Oblivion
4. Leading Brilliantly – The Fine Art of Personal and Organization Effectiveness
5. The Man Who Fell Too Far

Advance Praise for *The Man Who Fell Too Far*

We who live for the opportunity to devour a new book – as we might an exquisitely prepared favorite meal – this latest from Roger Corea is a page turner of the first order. Enjoy…or Bon Appetite!

Jack Benjamin

The Man Who Fell Too Far is a story of true friendships and intrigue. A real mystery that had me guessing until the end who done it! Roger Corea develops his characters in a way that makes you really care about them and want them to succeed. A real pleasurable and exciting read!

Robin Kukla

A psychological mystery thriller that tears a small town in the Adirondacks apart and delves into the deep-rooted secrets that bind them together. A lot of unexpected twists and turns that kept me riveted from beginning to end.

Lawrence Cilento

As with all Roger Corea's books, I was taken by his ability to paint a picture and have the reader enter that world, kind of like the rabbit hole in Alice In Wonderland. I thoroughly enjoyed his most recent undertaking.

Robert Tobin

Surprising twists and turns to this plot that takes place in Upstate New York, as well as some valuable insightful dialogue that could only be authored by an introspective intellect.

Susan Rice

The Man Who Fell Too Far is not only a psychological thriller that will keep you guessing until the very end, but a story about the emotional abuse of a child and his mother that will pull at your heart. A tangled web of destruction of a successful business man, the murder of the woman he loves, and his attempt to save his best friend from self-destruction are all wrapped up into one gripping thriller. Two men on a tense roller coaster ride of intrigue that keeps you on the edge of your seat wondering *who fell too far*.

Mary Jane Blum

I love thrillers! *The Man Who Fell Too Far* is one of the best! Half way through the novel I thought I had it all figured out. Boy, was I wrong. Usually, as an avid reader, I finish a novel in a month or so. This novel was different. I couldn't put it down and finished it in two days! I highly recommend this novel to anyone looking for an exciting reading experience!

Larry Wiese

Once in a while I come across a stimulating reading experience that I want to share with my friends and colleagues. *The Man Who Fell Too Far* is a thriller I would place in that category. The author's ability to portray the internal emotions of the characters was absolutely brilliant!

Rob O'Neil

TABLE OF CONTENTS

ACKNOWLEDGEMENTS

My sincere gratitude is extended to Mary Jane Blum and Robert Tobin for their excellent editorial advice. Their sharp insights, tedious efforts, and continuous reinforcement were extremely meaningful and very much appreciated.

CHAPTER ONE

May 1995 – Schroon Lake – Adirondack Mountains

As the last light of the northern sun began to fade, dusk silently turned to nightfall and soon everything in the forest would be hidden. A small rabbit chased by a red fox scampered across a one-lane mountain road. Both disappeared into a jungle of tall pines unaware of the shattered body of a man struggling to move to the side of the road.

The man's head pounded with pain. Blood saturated his face and limbs. Agony consumed his entire body. Despite his horrific condition, he feared the many eighteen-wheel logging trucks barreling down the road at breakneck speeds would not see him in the evening shadows. They would surely mistake him for ordinary road kill and not stop. I'm a dead man, he thought. He closed his eyes and lapsed into a state of unconsciousness.

Only an hour earlier, Jeff Walden made the final cable connection to a forty-foot utility pole near Schroon Lake in the Adirondack Mountains. He loved his job and understood the danger, yet prided himself on earning fat weekly paychecks, sometimes as much as four thousand dollars for four days' work.

But installing cables and telephone lines was treacherous and required teamwork and coordination. Typically, the minimum crew had one person monitoring the pulling equipment, one monitoring the supply reel, and one coordinating all involved in the installation. But now, with the setting sun, the teamwork had vanished. Jeff's workmates quit early, heading for the Schroon Lake beer gardens for a little TGIF. It was not his style to leave a job unfinished. So, he remained using a truck with a telescopic boom lift, known also as a "cherry picker". But Jeff forgot to check one critically important safety precaution: the chocks that go under the wheels that prevent the truck from rolling.

In the mysterious realm of human behavior, Jeff Walden would certainly be considered an anomaly. Obsessively independent, the closer he was to West Bumfuck, as he called it, the better off he was. He thrived on being isolated–wanting to be around other people only at his discretion. And, he arranged his life accordingly: equal parts work, drinking, playing the lottery, and fishing.

Never one to embrace the classroom learning process, he loved to quote Mark Twain's adage: Never let your book learnin' interfere with your education. But everything and anything interfered with his education.

A few years ago, after an altercation with the high school principal, Jeff was hauled off to the Hampton Farms Reformatory in Orange County, NY. It seems the principal didn't appreciate Jeff bringing a bottle of vodka to home economics class to make Bloody Mary's. He appreciated it even less when he poured a quart of tomato juice down the teacher's blouse. "How dare you…you little…", she hollered while a bright red spicy liquid dripped from her breasts. When the principal intervened, he ended up in the hospital with a broken jaw for his troubles. His punishment lasted one year and the only thing he had to show for it was the "Festus" moniker given to him by one of the guards.

People who knew Jeff agreed that the "Festus" tag was a pretty good fit. "Festus" was the thin, scruffy deputy on the popular television series "Gunsmoke". Almost everything about Jeff resembled Festus including his long black "Abraham Lincoln beard" that somehow made him look apostolic. But he was anything but apostolic. Pig-headed and defiant, yes, apostolic, no. And when anyone challenged the length of his shrub, he retorted, "Beards keep you warm, beards look cool, and beards store food for you. And what the hell is it to you anyway?"

But Jeff had even more incongruities. Not only was his beard long, but his tangled black mane looked like it was combed with a pitch fork. A worn-out baseball cap soaked with seagull guano concealed his unruly dome. Shabby jeans, ripped to the threads at the knees, and a solid black t-shirt, complemented his maverick attire. An ever-present hard pack of Marlboro's rolled up in his t-shirt sleeve exposed an eye-catching hairy brown birthmark on his upper arm. One night, while in a drunken stupor at the Bridgetown carnival, he had a tattoo artist etch some limbs around it making it look like an angry tarantula. By keeping his sleeve rolled up to his shoulder, Jeff joked that he could scare off pests, especially human ones. Despite his oddities, Jeff was highly regarded around Bridgetown. Known for his unselfishness and his trustworthiness, he was always willing to lend a hand at charitable events, especially those pertaining to the impoverished members of the community.

CHAPTER TWO

May 1995 – Schroon Lake – Adirondack Mountains

Michael Alexander finished dinner with his family at 8:15 p.m. at the rustic Witherbee's Carriage House, his favorite restaurant on Schroon Lake in the Adirondack Mountains. His new top of the line white 1995 BMW 740i sedan was waiting near the front door.

After tipping the valet, he and his family headed south to their summer vacation home, a five-bedroom palatial estate on four wooded acres of beach front property. His wife, Megan and their two children, Teddy and Jason, loved to vacation in Schroon Lake, but the summer season was passing quickly; they had to get back to Bridgetown this coming September for the start of school.

Michael Alexander was Jeff Walden's best friend. He first met Jeff at Luigi's, a local breakfast hangout in Bridgetown. Sitting at the counter, wolfing down four scrambled eggs, a mound of pancakes, and a healthy piece ham, Jeff was engaged in a spirited debate with Chief of Police, Lefty Margolis over whether O.J. Simpson "really did it".

"He's innocent!" Jeff asserted. "There was a serial killer loose in the neighborhood. He's the one who did it!"

"You're full of blueberries!" Lefty retorted. "Just look at the evidence! He used to beat her up all the time."

"That doesn't mean he killed her, Lefty!"

When Michael entered the restaurant, he hopped up on the stool and squeezed in next to Jeff. His first thought was he would now have breakfast with some homeless guy donning a baseball cap soaked with seagull guano. It was okay. Michael was the gregarious flexible type.

But Jeff was irked by the crowded nature at the counter and "accidentally" jounced Michael with his elbow spilling his coffee all over his freshly pressed blue business suit.

"Nice to meet you too!" Michael said with a good-natured smile.

"Oh! Pardon me. I'm so sorry," Jeff said feigning sincerity. "I didn't see you."

How the hell could he not see me, I was right next to him. "No problem. Have another cup of coffee on me?" Michael said chuckling. "Pun intended."

"No, no, no. I'll buy!" Jeff said attempting to ease the situation.

"Wait a minute!" Lefty declared. "I'm buyin' for you both!"

"Great idea! Let's allow Lefty buy!" Jeff said with a smile wanting to seize the opportunity of the moment.

"Thanks Lefty," Michael said laughing. "Boy, am I glad I came in here today!"

There was a short pause as the waitress served them breakfast.

"My God! Did you guys see the news today?" Lefty asked.

"Not yet but I'm sure we're gonna hear about it now," Jeff replied.

"Did you know O.J. was planning on getting married again?" Lefty asked.

"Seriously? I can't believe that!" Jeff answered.

"Yeah, he's gonna take another stab at it!" Lefty practically fell off the stool he was laughing so hard.

But Jeff wasn't the least bit entertained. He didn't even crack a smile. "How come you ain't laughing, Festus? I think that's hilarious."

"I just don't think it's at all funny."

Lefty shrugged his shoulders, smiled and said, "Festus, you ain't got no sense of humor, Man!"

"Maybe not," Jeff said. "I just don't think there's anything funny about two people getting slashed to death."

Michael was impressed with Jeff's self-control. He thought to himself, most people would have found some kind of diabolical pleasure from such a joke. Jeff simply stood his ground and maintained his values. This was the first occasion where he noticed something special about Jeff.

Over the years, Jeff and Michael's relationship blossomed. Michael hated doing what he considered menial maintenance chores around the house. He cringed when Megan asked him to fix anything. But most of the time he felt guilty because he knew he was neglecting his responsibilities and he didn't want to disappoint her.

Jeff, on the other hand, excelled at electrical, plumbing, and carpentry work. While he hated to paint, he was very meticulous with a paint brush. So, Michael hired Jeff part-time and was rescued from any further domestic "discomfort".

They enjoyed many of the same things. Michael shared Jeff's love of the Adirondacks, the spectacular view of Fort Ticonderoga, Lake Champlain and the surrounding area. Mount Defiance was their favorite place to unwind. Michael relished the escape from the pressures and demands of owning a thriving financial services firm in Bridgetown, which he started fourteen years ago right after he and Megan were married.

Michael was raised by a family of modest means that had high expectations. Successful attorneys flourished in his extended family and his parents, especially his mother, expected him to follow suit. Michael accepted his mother's wishes until he graduated from Villanova with a major in English literature. The thought of spending three more years in law school was anathema to Michael so he decided to teach high school English in Bridgetown instead.

Whether real or imagined, Michael assumed his parents were displeased with his career choice, believing he took the easy way out, not that they ever openly expressed their displeasure, but Michael always had a sixth sense about reading people. His empathic skills allowed him to understand nonverbal communication. This would serve him well later in his life.

But more importantly, there was a compelling motivation inside Michael that made him believe he could favorably influence students' behavior through the study of literature.

Teaching English Literature to high school students, Michael was a catalyst for spirited discussions on the subject of human fallibility—by challenging the main character's behavior, especially his or her flaws. How the main character handled the "struggle", he believed, was analogous to the inevitable struggles students would face during their lifetime.

By vicariously experiencing the plight of the main character, Michael believed huge learning opportunities would evolve. He asked them: "How will Holden Caufield, in Catcher in the Rye, overcome his rebellious and self-destructive attitude toward society? Will Lennie, in Of Mice and Men, overcome his addiction to extreme cruelty? How will Elizabeth, in The Crucible survive accusations of being a witch?"

In each case, how these characters dealt with their personal conflicts, not only revealed the depth of their character, but offers a significant learning opportunity for students.

"Think about it, Michael said, "are we not the main characters of our own life's story? Are we not the authors of our own destiny? Why not make our story a best seller? We are not perfect specimens of humanity. We all confront conflict daily. We succeed and fail. Our problems are small and large. How we cope with them, what we do about them, really determines our character as well as our overall satisfaction and happiness. The only mechanism I know to build character is the struggle. The struggle to overcome an adversity, the struggle to do the right thing when the wrong thing is easier and more popular, the struggle to cope with a myriad of life's difficulties and challenges, and the desire to sacrifice something meaningful for someone else. In many cases, the more formidable the struggle, the more impact there is the on someone's character."

The students elected Michael their MET (most effective teacher) three years in a row. He was extremely proud to have been selected, not necessarily because of his own personal achievement, but because he realized he must have been effective teaching his student's life management skills.

After his third year of teaching, much to the disappointment of students and teachers, Michael decided to "author his own destiny" by changing careers. Many people thought he was "lured" away from teaching for financial reasons. While more money certainly played a role in his decision, especially because of Michael's growing family responsibilities. However, the same compelling motivations inside Michael that made him believe he could favorably influence students, made him believe he could favorably influence adults. Instead of teaching life management skills, he would teach financial management skills.

As Michael and his family continued their drive to his summer home, he felt the obscurity of the Adirondack highlands. There were no street lights, guard rails, or street signs. It was a bad decision to have those two Martinis at the restaurant, he thought. For him to concentrate on the road, even with his bright lights on, was arduous and he was getting drowsy. He started to yawn and think about the clients who eagerly awaited his return to Bridgetown.

Teddy and Jason, new comers to the video game generation, were in the back seat playing Super Mario on their Nintendo Game Boys. Megan was thinking about some of the projects that needed completion at the lake. "I think I'll call Jeff," she said, "I'd like him to come over tomorrow and help finish the dock."

Then they heard a siren. It was getting louder and closer. Michael kept looking in the rearview mirror for flashing red lights of an emergency vehicle.

"You should move to the side of the road," Megan suggested. As he slowed down, a speeding patrol car passed by them followed by an ambulance.

"Look Michael! They both stopped up ahead – right in the middle of the road!"

"I don't see any other cars around," Megan said. "Wonder what the heck happened." She paused thoughtfully for a moment. "Michael! Hasn't Jeff been working in this area all week?"

"My God, that's right!"

Michael drove slowly to the scene, carefully making sure he didn't impede the first responders rushing to the center of the road. When he stopped, and stepped out of his car, bright red road flares nearly blinded his view. He struggled to see a body in the middle of the road. He approached an officer stationed a few feet from the ambulance who was blocking traffic. "Excuse me officer. What happened here," he asked.

"Some guy working on the lines fell out of the canopy and landed on the pavement. He probably forgot to chock the tires on his truck. He's unconscious and in pretty bad shape." Michael darted to the area where the medics were working.

He could see Jeff's unconscious body sprawled on the asphalt in a pool of blood. Three medics in white coats were kneeled around him giving him oxygen and administering other life support procedures.

"How bad is it?" he frantically asked one of the medics. He almost didn't want to hear the answer.

The medic stood up with a distressed look and slowly shook his head. "It's a serious head injury. A trucker in an eighteen-wheeler, the one parked down the road there, just missed running over him. He's the one that called 911."

"Where are you taking him?" Michael asked.

"Moses Ludington Hospital in Ticonderoga."

"It's about twenty miles away, isn't it?" Michael queried. "Nothing closer?"

"It's the best trauma care hospital in the area and I am afraid he's going to need all the help he can get."

Michael hurried back to the car. "It's Jeff!" he exclaimed. "He tumbled out of the 'cherry picker' and landed on his head. He's in really bad shape, honey."

"I knew it!" Megan cried. "This was an accident waiting to happen. Well, you know, honey, every day after three, it's a ritual. He has to have that goddamn beer."

"Unfortunately, you're right." Michael said, "he has to play the lottery too. I'll bet he went into town for lunch, played his numbers, and came back with a six pack. Then when he moved the truck he forgot to chock the wheels. It's an easy mistake to make."

"Not when your sober it isn't!" Megan countered. "And Michael, there is no such thing as a six-pack for Jeff. He only buys twelves!"

"Is Jeff dead?" a frightened Jason asked. His eyes, like tennis balls, his heart beating so fast, it was like a drum roll. Jeff was his pal.

"I'm afraid he's badly hurt, buddy," Megan said, who was sobbing and clearly distraught. "Where are they taking him?"

"To Moses," Michael replied. "I'll take you and the kids home then I'm going over there. I'll be home when I find out how badly the poor guy is hurt."

CHAPTER THREE

May 1995 – Moses Ludington – Ticonderoga

After Michael dropped off his family at their home, he sped to Moses Ludington in Ticonderoga. On his way, he reflected on the times Jeff and his boys camped on top of Mt. Defiance. Fort Ticonderoga and the hospital were in clear view from their camp site. How ironical he thought. Defiance…it was the perfect word to describe Jeff's personality.

The last time they camped there, he remembered Jeff scurrying around the woods accumulating tinder. He would brag that no one could build a campfire like he could. And, he was right. At first, the flames ascended high into the sky–too intense to get near, but the intoxicating smell of musky smoke and pine needles were so beguiling they couldn't wait for the fire to calm. As it crackled and simmered, the boys went into their olive-green Army tent and brought out plastic bags full of fat white marshmallows. They carved short twigs to pierce them and then assumed comfortable positions around the fire and began roasting.

Michael watched as Jeff stood motionless, transfixed by the alluring site of Fort Ticonderoga as if he himself had participated in the battle there more than 200 years ago.

"He took the fort without any causalities, British or American. He took the fort!" Jeff reiterated. "It was the first American victory of the Revolutionary War which gave the Army artillery to drive the British out of Boston. You know," he said despondently, "Benedict Arnold was a true American hero."

"That's not right," Teddy said. "Mr. Marcum, my history teacher, told our class he was a dirty rat and betrayed his own country." He pulled a marshmallow from a plastic bag and skewered it on the sharp end of a twig then gently placed it near the fire.

"He was screwed by congress!" Jeff thundered. "Them freakin' teachers… they ain't got a clue. They don't know what the hell they are talking about. I would have damn well done the same thing! I would have wasted that goddamn wimpy George Washington too!"

"Don't you like America, Jeff?" Teddy asked with a subtle but serious smile.

"It's the freakin' government… it sucks! They're all a bunch of crooks who line their pockets and sit on their butts and do nothin' all day. I told the mayor straight up to fix the stupid potholes all over town. You know what happened to Butch Donatello?"

"No," Teddy said, "but I'll bet we are going to find out right now!" Jason and Teddy both giggled as they gazed at the fire and turned their marshmallows.

"Well, listen to this! On his way to a construction job, he broke an axle on his pick-up truck and now he is tryin' to get the town to pay for the repairs. Good luck with that!" Jeff scoffed. "When he finally got to the job, the owner was so pissed off he fired him. Who's gonna to pay Butch for all the money he lost on that job? Not the town…that's for sure! If it were me, I'd sue all those freakin' idiots! And don't get me goin' about the garbage problem!"

"But what about Benedict Arnold?" Teddy persisted. "Isn't he really a traitor?"

"He was a hero! Listen to me! Don't believe that crap them teachers feed you in school about him being a traitor! Washington and the Continental Congress–they didn't know nothin'. They kept recognizin' everyone else but him. Then that dumb ass General Gates–he took all the glory for winning the battle of Saratoga even though Arnold led the battle and even got shot in the leg. And those Sons of Liberation or Liberty, or maybe a better name – Sons of bitches–whatever…he was one of them! In fact, he started them! He was a great soldier and if it weren't for him we'd all be British right now!"

Jason raised his eyebrows. He knew Jeff well and that he was prone to long-winded tangents and irrational prejudices. He asked Jeff, "So, just because the congress didn't like him he became a traitor? Sounds like sour grapes to me."

"Sour grapes, huh?" Jeff said now visibly agitated. He stood up and moved away from the fire as if he needed space to wigwag. "Well, it's like this," he shrugged waving his arms in the air, "When he was in Philadelphia, he liked to gamble and play the horses just like me. Can't fault him for that, can we?"

"He probably lost all his money," Teddy guessed before he devoured another burnt marshmallow. "Ah! This one's hot!"

Michael finally spoke up, "Arnold got hoodwinked by the British."

"Well… yeah," Jeff admitted. But it wasn't his fault. The British set him up and he got himself a huge gamblin' debt. Then he got sucked in by some 19-year-old bimbo who just happened to be loyal to the British. The British took advantage of him when he was drunk and bribed him with gold. He had no freakin' choice. Tell me…what would you guys do?"

"I wouldn't betray my own country for anything!" Teddy said, who just finished his third marshmallow.

"Me neither!" Jason agreed. I'll bet if they caught him, he would go to jail for a long time."

Quiet through most of the conversation, Michael could no longer maintain his silence. "Look Jason and Teddy," he said kindheartedly, "I have to tell you that Jeff is quite good at history, but he left out one critical fact. Washington put Benedict Arnold in charge of West Point but then Arnold offered it to the British along with access to our secret military information."

"Cool move!" Jeff asserted. "They deserved it!"

"No, Jeff, that was a horrible move!" Michael countered. "I don't want you guys to believe that Benedict Arnold was some kind of super hero. Jeff has most of his facts correct, but it is his allegiance that gives me pause."

"So, what the heck happened to Arnold, Dad?" Jason asked.

"The British Colonel who was negotiating the spy deal with Arnold, I think his name was John Andre, was caught with evidence of Arnold's defection and Arnold jumped on a ship heading for Britain. But the British never trusted him."

"Ah! C'mon you guys! Give me a break! Arnold got a raw deal!" Jeff was infuriated. He walked away from the fire and disappeared into the woods not to be seen until the next morning.

"So much for Jeff and his American history lesson," Michael said with a cackle. "I'm knocked out and going to bed. Goodnight Jason. Goodnight Teddy."

"Goodnight, Dad. Don't let the sleeping bag bugs bite," Teddy said.

"Hey guys, it's time for you to hit the rack too!"

When Michael arrived at the Moses Ludington emergency room, he approached the nurse at the reception desk. "I am a close friend of Jeff Walden's. May I go back and see how he is?"

"I'm sorry, only relatives are allowed," she responded. "Damn. I should have lied." "I'm really the only 'family' he has. Can you at least tell me his condition?"

"I'll be happy to check on him for you. Please have a seat over there," she said pointing to the waiting area.

That was fine with Michael. It was okay if she didn't return for a while; it had been a long and stressful evening. He placed his elbow on the armrest of the chair, slouched down with his hand supporting his forehead. He closed his eyes and exhaled. Maybe I could just nap for a few minutes. However, he could not stop worrying about Jeff. How bad were his injuries? Would he ever recover? Who is going to take care of him when and if he is released? And, what about medical costs? He knew Jeff refused to pay health insurance premiums because of his disdain for insurance companies. For God's sake. The last time Jeff saw a doctor was in the delivery room when he was born! I'm not going to worry about that now. If need be, I'll pay for his medical expenses. The important thing is that he gets better.

Michael's ruminations were interrupted by a pleasing female voice. "Hi. My name is Marci. I'm Dr. Rheingold's, PA. Are you Mr. Walden's next of kin?"

"Yes, you could say that." Michael rose from his chair to maintain eye contact and introduce himself. "Thank you for finding me," he said graciously.

"Well, Mr. Walden is in surgery. The doctor told me to tell you his condition is 'delicate'."

Michael winced. "'Delicate' as in 'critical'?"

"I'm sorry, but yes."

"How extensive are his injuries?"

"Well, for starters, he has a fractured skull. The doctor is operating right now to alleviate pressure on his brain. There are a few fractured vertebrae. His left clavicle is also broken."

"Oh my God." Michael slowly collapsed back into the chair. What's the prognosis?"

She shook her head. "I'm afraid we won't know anything until after surgery. I realize these chairs are quite uncomfortable. My advice is that you go home and get some rest. I'll call you as soon as he comes out of surgery."

"Well, if you don't mind, I'll stay right here. My head is spinning; I'm not sure I can even drive. Could you please let me know when the surgery is complete?"

"Of course," she said with a gentle accepting smile.

"Thank you, Marci."

Michael was physically exhausted, but his mind was full speed ahead. All the little idiosyncrasies about his relationship with Jeff were coming to fore. He always accepted him for what he was while everyone else tried to overhaul his personality according to their standards of behavior. Sure, there were times when he was difficult to tolerate but it was impossible to dislike him. He had a big heart, like the many times he helped me deliver furniture and clothing to the needy and poor people of Bridgetown.

"Helping the poor is my ticket to heaven," he would say, and he wasn't joking. Michael remembered the kind things Jeff had done for him as well for others. His heart was always ready, willing, and able regardless of how difficult the job. When Jeff found Megan's, wallet buried under the front seat of his car with five hundred dollars of cash in it, he immediately returned it. Michael remembered when a bucket of paint accidentally fell off the fireplace mantel and landed on Megan's new couch and chair. Jeff cried like a baby and promised to pay for the damage. Fortunately, Megan was fond of Jeff and very forgiving of his foibles. She affectionately called him, The Redneck Philosopher.

She had good reason for that nickname. Jeff would preach to anyone within earshot and he purported to be an authority on everything. Not that he wasn't well-informed. It was amazing how much information Jeff's mind contained. He would just get hung up on the minor details, like believing Benedict Arnold was a hero, for instance.

Listening to the world according to Jeff was mostly entertaining but some people found it aggravating, especially when he launched into one of his many pet peeves.

For example, few people, especially Megan, could tolerate his incessant coaching while in a car…when to turn, when to stop…and he hated expressways and if you didn't follow his directions, an argument would ensue. His driver's license was suspended with a third DUI conviction several years ago but as a passenger he was incorrigible. "Jeff!" Michael once scolded him, "for a guy who hasn't driven in a decade, you sure are a pain in the ass in the car!" Of course, Jeff ignored him and never ended his tedious lecturing. Oddly, most of the time, he knew what he was talking about and never once in his entire life did he ever get lost.

"I know how to get to places!" he would argue. "I've worked all over the northeast! I don't like these new-fangled expressways and that dumb thing called GSS or GPS. New technology… it don't work worth a crap!"

"Maybe you should apply for a position with Rand McNally Road Maps," Michael once said to him facetiously. "Jeff, you really are an aggravating individual in a car."

Sometimes, Jeff wasn't sure how to perceive Michael's attitude. He thought he was providing meaningful driving assistance, most notably with Megan, who was a woman and he believed she really didn't know her way around the block. Even she seemed impatient with him. He simply could never understand why. But that was Jeff simply being Jeff.

Chapter Four

May 1995–Moses Ludington Hospital – Ticonderoga

Michael was getting restless. It was three in the morning and he had been in the reception area of Moses Ludington Hospital for at least four hours and still did not know if Jeff was going to live or die.

The sound of a loud buzzer startled him. Then he heard an announcement. "Dr. Rheingold to room 190 stat!" He tried to collect himself then called for a nurse. Just then, Marci returned.

"Hello Mr. Alexander. I have an update on Mr. Walden. You know, in these situations, there is always good and bad news." Michael braced himself. "The good news is that Mr. Walden is out of surgery. In most cases, the skull will protect the brain from serious harm. The bad news is that injuries as severe as Mr. Walden's can cause serious cognitive issues down the road."

"Don't worry. Mr. Walden has the hardest head in the Western Hemisphere. I can attest to that!" Michael couldn't help himself. As much as he was hurting inside, a little comic relief felt good.

Marci smiled. "I hear you," she said.

"I apologize. But you know what I mean, right?"

"Sure do! Actually, we don't think there was any brain damage, but his fractured skull will need a several weeks of complete bed rest to get better. His back will be painful, and he will need intensive therapy. He will go home with a bandage and staples and can remove the bandage when Dr. Rheingold tells him to… probably in a week or so… the staples in about three weeks."

"Mr. Alexander, keep in mind that he will have pain, and the area may be swollen for up to three to four months or so. The doctor will provide antibiotics and steroid medicine to decrease the swelling. Also, the pain may cause abnormal even bizarre behavior."

Michael sensed another opportunity to be witty but caught himself. "What does that mean?" he asked.

"His behavior will be erratic and unpredictable…it is just the nature of a bad head injury. Several weeks of rest and immobility are crucial."

"I heard on the intercom that there was an emergency in room 190. Did it have anything to do with Jeff?"

"Yes. It's unbelievable! He woke up and was determined to get out of bed. He wanted to leave."

"That's Jeff!" Michael quipped.

"The doctor attached a halo device which will keep him from moving his head and neck."

"He's no saint, you know!" Michael took another shot at humor.

"Yes, I have already come to that conclusion." Marci said delicately. "Halos are often used for skull fractures when the patient is not stable. He's a challenge. We've never seen anyone wake up so soon after surgery, let alone try to get out of bed."

"There must be a way to restrain him," Michael said, "like strapping him down to the bed, right? I know him. He'll try it again if he isn't somehow tied down."

"Well…the doctor just gave him some strong pain medicine, so he should be asleep pretty soon."

Michael shook his head. "The only thing that will put him to sleep is a couple of shots of rattlesnake venom… and I'm not too sure even that would work!"

"Listen…why don't you go home and come back later in the morning. There isn't anything you are going to accomplish sitting in this hard chair for another four hours. I am sure your friend is sleeping and when you come back you can speak with the doctor. Okay?"

Michael closed his eyes, stretched, and yawned broadly. "Yup. Good idea," he said. "See you later Marci and thanks very much for your help."

"No problem. Glad I could be of assistance."

After bidding farewell to Michael, Marci worked her way back to her small office adjacent to the nurse's station and not too far from Jeff's room. She sat down and began plowing through the mound of paperwork on her desk and at the same time wondered why Michael, a polished, articulate, and classy man, had such a strong connection to Jeff, a rather boorish, indigent man. No big deal, she thought…just seems so contrasting.

Suddenly, she was interrupted by earsplitting screams that could be heard all over the floor. She rushed to his room.

"Give me something stronger…please!" Jeff pleaded. He was on the verge of tears. She could hear the deep agony in his voice. Sleeping was impossible. His head felt like it was smashed with a crowbar.

"Nothing works for shit!" he screeched.

Marci looked at him woefully knowing there was nothing she could do. He begged her for morphine. "Jeff, I am sorry, she said. "But the doctor said, 'no morphine.' He thinks you are prone to seizures and, in your condition, just one seizure could be fatal."

"I'd rather be dead than have this pain!" he shouted. "Someone has to fuckin' do something!"

"I understand," she said soothingly and began rubbing his arm gently. "Try and think of something else." After a few minutes, he exhaled and closed his eyes. Then, with his eyes half open, he gazed curiously at the ceiling tiles.

"Whoever did those freakin' ceilin' tiles really screwed up," he moaned. "When I do ceilin' tiles, they have no nicks, no tears." He was right… they were flat as a granite counter and straight as a German razor. Jeff was a perfectionist.

Marci placed another pillow gently behind his head. "Thank you for taking good care of me," he said kindly. "Sorry I'm such a monster." He closed his eyes, and gradually fell into a shallow slumber, one that allowed him to rest but also reminisce.

Jeff saw himself high up in the cherry picker looking over the tall pines and seeing the lake in distance. He remembered looking for his boat but all he could see was the beach where it used to be. Did someone steal my boat? he wondered. His eyes scanned the lake, but he was too high up and far away to get a closer look at the many boats on the lake. Then he felt the wheels slip on the truck. Shit! Why is this thing moving? He remembered chocking the tires with wedged two by fours. "What the hell is going on?" He depressed the hydraulic down lever and the canopy began descending slowly. He didn't want to take any chances. Then the truck stopped moving. He waited a few minutes and then raised the lever, so the canopy rose back to where it was. He continued working as his thoughts evolved back to his boat. Maybe one of the neighbors borrowed the boat. Suddenly, the truck started to roll again. This time it picked up speed rolling downhill through a narrow path reserved for work vehicles. He was helpless. He could feel the branches thrash his face, arms, and body. His hard hat flew off when it was whipped by one of the larger branches. Now his head was exposed, and he thought about grabbing one the limbs and hanging on until someone could come for him. It was too late. The truck hit a tree head-on and Jeff was catapulted like a projectile shot from a cannon on to the hard pavement of the road below.

He opened his eyes slowly. For a fleeting moment, he was surprised how vivid his thoughts were of the accident, yet how sluggish his brain was now that he was awake. He felt agitated and angry. He attempted to roll over only to be restrained by wrist braces. Do they have to be so damn tight? Now he was really getting pissed off.

Michael could barely keep his eyes open when driving home. Not to awaken Megan, he collapsed on the family room couch. In the morning, Megan instructed the children not to disturb him.

The hours passed quickly and by the time Michael opened his eyes, it was noon. He scurried around the house finding his clothes. Once he arrived back at the hospital, he would insist on speaking with the doctor when he arrived.

Megan left a note saying that she was taking the children shopping for clothing and school supplies. She would be wanting to get back to Bridgetown soon. Also, several clients would be eager to see me. I've got to get back but in my heart of hearts I know I can't leave Schroon Lake unless I'm confident that Jeff is going to be okay.

When he arrived at Moses Ludington, the elevator door was already open as if it was inviting him in. When it closed, he said a short prayer for Jeff. On the next floor, a doctor with the name "Rheingold" on his name tag entered the elevator.

"Dr. Rheingold, I'm Mike Alexander, a very close friend of your patient, Jeff Walden."

"Oh yes. A stubborn young man for sure!" Dr. Rheingold smiled, but Michael was sure Dr. Rheingold already had Jeff figured out.

"Will he be okay?"

"Like I explained to him earlier this morning… everything depends on bed rest and a quiet environment to recuperate for a couple of months. Mr. Alexander, I should tell you, his injuries were quite severe. Not taking my advice – and by the way – my advice is non-negotiable–he may not survive." Dr. Rheingold spoke slowly, confidently, and matter-of-factly.

Immediately, Michael became more worried. "Keeping him down for a couple of months is a major stretch," he said. "Can you give him something?" Just then the elevator door opened, and they stepped out and continued the conversation in hallway.

"I could place him into a temporary coma," the doctor said. "A comatose brain needs less oxygen to function. I'm hesitant to do it just to keep him still, yet the pressure in his brain is certainly serious enough. But, no, I don't believe it is wise."

"I understand," Michael said.

"And then we have to contend with the possibility of blood clots. I'm afraid he could have some serious cognitive or reasoning issues if we don't keep close tabs on him. Oh, by the way, a Catholic priest came into his room this morning to give him Last Rites and he got very angry and started to holler so much that the priest left his room."

Michael sighed and shook his head. "Guess there won't be any angels calling."

"It's too bad. Jeff is really seriously injured," Dr. Rheingold lamented.

"So, what you are saying is he won't be installing any cable lines anytime soon, if ever."

"Indeed. I'm sorry," Dr. Rheingold conceded.

Michael thanked the doctor for his candid appraisal and proceeded directly to Jeff's room. Oddly, he felt somewhat relieved. At least now I have clarity, he thought. Although the expectations are challenging, Jeff's survival depends on taking direction from a doctor. Michael knew that would be a tall order. Any kind of direction or regimentation whatsoever was unbearable to Jeff.

The nurse's station was so busy, no one noticed Michael in the hallway, yet Michael noticed a covered body on a gurney being pushed by a rather obese orderly and thought nothing of it. Once inside Jeff's room, he walked to the bed. Something was in the bed, but it wasn't Jeff. It was the old pillow trick – the "pillow in the blanket trick"– pillows bunched vertically in the shape of a body to fool people from a distance. But Michael was up close. He was stunned and speechless.

"Oh, my God!" he erupted. His head shook in resignation. His first impulse was to search the lavatories and hallways. That's damn stupid! No one is going to find him if he doesn't want to be found. He obviously planned his getaway so what good would it do to look for him? Then again, he may be hiding on another floor. He pushed the emergency call button near the bed.

When Marci entered the room, she was totally befuddled and glared at the bed incredulously. "I can't believe this! she asserted. "I saw him fifteen minutes ago and he was out cold! Earlier, he complained about the pain and we medicated him with some pretty strong pain pills. There is no way he could walk out of here by himself.

He had to have some help. I'm calling security and have them check every floor and guard the exits."

While Marci's efforts were commendable, Michael knew Jeff well. He would never allow himself to be found inside the hospital. Jeff is long gone. It will take them forever to search the entire hospital and they will never find him. I'm leaving!

Michael was offended. Jeff was throwing mud in the faces of those who were trying to save his life. He told the nurse at the reception desk to call him should Jeff somehow materialize or if they learned anything about his whereabouts.

Against his better judgement, Michael traveled to at Jeff's cabin on Schroon Lake. I realize that finding Jeff here is a lot like finding Jimmy Hoffa selling Kool Aid in front of Luigi's. Jeff surely knew that his cabin would be the first place anyone would search.

Michael noticed his Pontiac Firebird was still in the driveway. Not that Jeff could drive it but, whoever helped him could. He walked slowly inside the one-story cabin searching for any clues.

Jeff was an impeccable housekeeper. He made Fussy Felix on the Odd Couple look like Stanley the dirt monkey. Today, however, the place was a wall-to-wall mess, but Michael didn't see anything unusual on the floor until his eyes zeroed in on the nightstand beside the bed. That .45 caliber snub nose that was always on his nightstand is gone! Michael's imagination went rampant with nefarious thoughts. Why the hell would Jeff want his pistol?

As Michael continued his inspection of the premises, he walked out the back and noticed the padlock on the old icebox was missing. He knew Jeff hid his money there. He opened the icebox looking for a burlap bag and found it empty.

Where the hell is the boat? Impossible! No goddamn way Jeff could be out fishing so soon after the accident.

Michael called the New York State Police number on the phone inside the cabin. They patrolled the lake daily, enforcing navigation laws and providing search and rescue services. He recalled that Jeff was no stranger to the New York State Police. When I tell them the name of the person lost, they just might perceive it as their lucky day. At any rate, it was going to be a long day. When he explained the urgency of the situation, the officer responded with one of those long, slow, unconvincing "Well…ohhh kaaay." They don't believe me. I don't blame them. It is simply too outrageous to imagine.

Driving up and down the coast for a few hours hoping to spot Jeff's boat was useless. Michael was convinced, in his condition, Jeff could never operate his boat. Another person had to be helping him and the boat was probably hidden in some cove. He certainly wouldn't be cruising the open seas where someone could easily spot him during daylight hours. The son of a bitch is probably fishing and having a grand ole' time! Michael snickered to himself. It was funny but not really that funny at all. Michael returned home weary and exasperated.

"I feel like Chingachgook tracking Natty Bumppo!" Michael said to Megan when he walked through the door. "If he doesn't want to be found, the hell with him! I've about had it with the pain in the ass!"

"Michael," Megan said. "Jeff's a big boy… albeit a senseless big boy…but we both know that no one is going to control him. Not you, not me, not even a doctor who is trying to save his life."

"His boat was gone! Do you believe that? So were his clothes and his money from that broken-down icebox…his gun too!

"Hmm…Megan paused a few seconds. "I don't believe it."

"What do you mean?"

"I think the boat disappearing is just another one of his maneuvers…a diversionary tactic designed to change the scent. You remember how cagy he is?"

Michael instantly recalled the pillow in the blanket trick that Jeff pulled in the hospital. That thought strengthened the notion he was serious about not being found.

Wait minute! What about that gurney that passed me in the hallway? Michael closed his eyes shaking his head in disgust. Maybe that was Jeff under the sheets!

Megan was getting edgy. "You know, at this point, honey, there isn't anything more you can do about the situation and we need to get back to our life in Bridgetown. The kids have summer projects and if you don't get back to service your clients soon they're going to move all their money to Freddy over at Flintstone's Financial Services."

"Freddy?" Michael smiled. He was only slightly amused at Megan's admirable attempt at humor. "Yeah. I know."

Inside, however, he felt an uncomfortable emptiness. Although it was altogether illogical, he felt he was abandoning Jeff. Nonetheless, his own family and livelihood came first. He knew that and agreed to leave for Bridgetown later that afternoon.

"Michael…you know what? I think he's back in Bridgetown visiting his son, Tyler."

Chapter Five

Schroon Lake–June 1990–Five Years Earlier

Jeff was ecstatic. After a few years of breathing coal dust in a West Virginia coal mine, he was offered his dream job in a remote area of the Adirondack Mountains as a lineman hanging telephone cable.

There were good reasons for his ecstasy. The Adirondacks were the perfect location for Jeff to implement his passion for fishing. The landlocked Salmon and Smallmouth were large and plentiful in Schroon Lake. His first two days off each week were spent fishing and bar hopping. His third day was spent sleeping and sobering up…the perfect schedule for an unattached young man.

The problem was that Jeff, on paper, if not in practice, was "attached". But Jeff lived the carefree life of a single man. Instead of chasing women, he chased the most seductive fishing spots he could find. Schroon Lake was at the top of his list.

One Saturday at five in the morning, unable to sleep, he sat up in his bed and remembered the minnow bucket full of fresh shiners he tied to the dock. Why bother with breakfast? he asked himself. He grabbed his fishing gear and proceeded out the door to his fourteen-foot fishing boat beached on the sandy shore behind his small cabin hideaway. A slight push on hull and the boat was afloat. The small

Evinrude came to life with one gentle pull of the starter cord. The lake was smooth as glass reflecting a kaleidoscope of brilliant colors beckoning him to get out there and put a line in the water. He pointed the boat to an island across the bay called the Garden of Eden. It was his favorite fishing spot.

Jeff loved the feel of the cool morning wind blowing into his face. The pristine, unblemished nature of the island always improved his mood and provided a sense of seclusion, the feeling that he was in a faraway place, away from people that aggravated him, and most of them did. He could see the gulls drifting endlessly in the wind, appearing not to have a care in the world. All his pressures and worries were evaporating, his responsibilities suddenly erased. He wondered if he would see his friend, "Eli", the thousand-pound bull moose swimming back to the mainland after an evening of browsing for food on the island.

Jeff eased up on the throttle about ten yards out from the island. A partially submerged fallen tree looked like a good place to tie up. Behind the tree was the well-camouflaged polyester duck blind he constructed last summer. It blended perfectly with the woodland scenery on the island. Roasted Duck will be on the menu when hunting season opens.

He began casting into a cluster of water lilies, but it was difficult for him to concentrate. Whenever Jeff fished the Garden of Eden shoreline, his eight-year-old son, Tyler, dominated his thoughts. He looked forward to the day when Tyler could join him, and they could murder the bass together. If I keep bustin' my ass as a line jockey and keep my nose clean, he mused, I just might be able to pay college costs for Tyler. It doesn't have to be one of those phony hot shit Ivy League schools where folks pay thousands of dollars in tuition, so their kid

can use fifty cent words. A small two-year college would be good–
something I never had. Despite his frequent absences from his family,
that possibility made Jeff feel very good about himself. It provided a
significant goal, something worth working to achieve. He loved his
son more than anything else in world.

It was late morning. The early morning chill had been replaced
by warm rays of sunlight that glistened on the water like dancing
diamonds. The fish were biting, so with a full stringer of Smallmouth
Bass, he decided to call it day and cruise back to his cabin.

Once there, he gave the place a quick once over and noticed his
trusty Smith & Wesson snub nosed pistol was still on the nightstand
near his bed, just where he expected it to be.

He backed up his refurbished 1976 Pontiac Firebird Trans Am, his
most treasured possession, to a ramshackle ice box near the back door
of his cabin. After unlocking a padlock, he lifted out two burlap bags:
one filled with hundred-dollar bills and the other with his plentiful
catch of smallmouth. He tossed both bags into the trunk of his car
and drove off to Ray's Fish Shack located in the middle of downtown
Schroon Lake.

Ray Bach, a long-time resident of the Schroon Lake area and
a well-respected business owner, grudgingly tolerated a few strange
characters hanging out in his short order restaurant. Jeff supplied Ray
with a plethora of salmon and bass which Ray sold to his customers.
As compensation, he often prepared Jeff's meals without charge.

Walking through the front door, Jeff tossed the burlap bag filled
with fish on the kitchen floor next to Ray. "Let's choke these bad boys
down when I get back tomorrow. That's if I can get the hell back here
before midnight!" Ray quietly picked up the bag and placed it in the
flat-top freezer behind the bar.

"Hey numb nuts!" echoed a loud voice from the back of the room, "You ain't back by six, I'll choke those puppies down myself! So, you best get your ass back here early, boy!"

Joey "The Snork" Esposito, the resident pinball junkie and drunk, was playing Street Fighter on the pinball machine and eavesdropping at the same time. A big man with a large belly, he had to stand two feet back from the machine to operate it. The "Snork" had to play pinball with his left hand because his right hand was supposedly bitten off by a bull shark while he was snorkeling in the Florida Keys, the origin of the "Snork" moniker.

"Well, well, well," Jeff said. "If it ain't the one and only Mr. Lead-in-the- Ass! Listen up you drunken rummy. By the time I get back, you'll be too damned shitfaced to walk let alone eat!"

The Snork shuffled his three-hundred-pound frame in Jeff's direction. Ray was frying eggs behind the counter. "Bring it on fat man!" Jeff shouted. Worried that his recent investment in new tables and bar stools might be trashed, Ray suddenly darted from behind the counter and stood between them before they came to blows.

"Knock it off!" he said loudly, as he pushed them away from each other. "Listen dip-shits! It's not okay to bust up my joint again! If you can't respect my place of business, then you ain't welcome here! You hear me?"

"Oh yeah, sorry, Ray," Snork said with the sincerity of a snake oil salesman. He extended his left hand to Jeff to shake and make peace. Welcoming this apparent friendly gesture, Jeff stretched out his left-hand arm to comply but then Snork pulled it away at the last second and said with a condescending grin, "Festus! What the hell makes you think I want to be your friend?"

A confused frown crossed Jeff's face. He felt slighted as fits of hilarity overcame the place and someone yelled, "Hey Snork, you really got to hand it to him." Being the brunt of someone else's joke was unbearable, especially from his long-standing on again off again antagonistic friend.

"Okay!" Ray said, smiling and relieved that the impending fisticuffs had passed.

"So, Festus, tell me, what is on your agenda for the day."

"I think I am going to Bridgetown to visit the little man and Francine, his poor excuse for a mother." Jeff couldn't conceal his regret; it was written all over his face.

"How old is that 'little man' now?" Ray asked as he broke three eggs with one hand. "He's about ready for a fishing trip ain't he?" Ray turned around and slid a cup of coffee in front of Jeff.

"Seven. Can't wait to educate the kid how to fish. He's a bit young for that now but sometime maybe next year…if I can yank him away from his old lady."

"Well, there's always a silver lining. My wife dumped me years ago for the Seagram's Liquor salesman and it was the best thing that ever happened to me, although I didn't think so at the time. She had a humongous drug problem. And that led to other issues, you know… sleepin' around and alcohol. She was blitzed every goddamn day of the week! That kind of addiction is the worst kind of disease."

"Yeah. Tell me about it. I worry about Francine for that same reason. She's always miserable and never strays too far from the goddam cocaine. Someday, I am going to go through that freakin' house and find all that shit and flush it down the toilet. Then I'm gonna take her to the wellness clinic and lock her up!"

"Good luck with that. Can you get her to agree to go?"

"Probably not. But I really care about what's gonna happen to my son, Tyler…you know…being around a druggie. He sees her out of her mind blitzed all the time and I'm very suspicious about her sexual habits. Plus, my idiot brother, Billy, sleeps there."

Ray shook his head. "Not a good situation… it just ain't right,"

"Thanks Ray." As Jeff finished his eggs and ham, he looked over at the pinball machine. "Hey Snorkus Eliptus," he shouted. "Keep it in your pants…that's if you can ever find it."

"Up yours, Festus! Drop in again sometime when you can't stay! Or, better yet, just drop dead!" Snork waved then got back to his pinball.

CHAPTER SIX

June 1990–Bridgetown

After leaving Ray's, Jeff proceeded south to Albany, then headed west to Bridgetown, a small municipality of about six thousand residents. His wife, Francine and son, Tyler, resided there for the last eight years, after they moved up from Morgantown, West Virginia.

Bridgetown was unique among Upstate New York towns having the only downhill lift bridge in the world. It spanned the Erie Canal right in the middle of town. Jeff operated the bridge during his teenage years from an archaic white and brown wooden tower about twenty-five feet high. However, one day after a few too many brewskies, Jeff confused the up and down switches on the control panel. A beautiful double decker 50-foot Sea Ray Sundancer, as it passed under the bridge, quickly became a beautiful single decker Sea Ray Sundancer. That's when Jeff's bridge lifting career came to a crunching halt.

Jeff enjoyed recalling experiences like that of his youth, especially when he was behind the wheel of his prized Firebird. He grabbed the Marlboro hard pack tucked in his T-shirt sleeve and began a smoking marathon that would not end until he reached Bridgetown.

The high-pitched whine of the Firebird's engine was like a Carnegie Hall concert to Jeff. It lowered his stress, elevated his mood, and fueled his thought processes.

Gratitude for his high paying job was his first thought. His second was how fortunate he was to spend so much of his time fishing. It was certainly much better than my last job digging for coal in Morgantown. I was always afraid of being crushed to death or being burned to death by the exploding gas or blown to hell and back by a blast of dynamite.

That job was physically brutal. His hands became cut and scarred by the sharp pieces of slate and coal, while his finger nails were worn to the quick from contact with the iron chute. The air he breathed, saturated with coal dust, congested his lungs and he coughed for days on end. The summers were fiercely hot and the winters bitterly cold. I saw enough crippled miners with lung disease to know, sooner or later, I had to get the hell out.

Then there was Carmela. Jeff recalled the night he met Carmela at Crockett's Lodge in Morgantown. She was a Freshman at West Virginia University and certainly not the sharpest knife in the drawer. In fact, many wondered how she even got into the drawer in the first place. But she was smokin' hot! And that's all I cared about. I mean like she was beggin' for it too! I didn't want to take advantage of her but drinking that goddamn cheap Wild Irish Rose Wine crap, she had really got me tanked, especially when she forced me to guzzle the whole freakin' bottle! That girl had it all… long beautiful legs that wouldn't quit…tits that would make grown men cry. I couldn't help myself, but getting laid that night was great, but it was a horrible mistake! She talked me into to moving into her dorm room with three other girls. It seemed like a great idea at the time. We dated for three months. But she was the moodiest bitch I ever met…domineering too! And what a freakin' drama queen. She was always cryin' or bitchin' about something. I couldn't deal with it. Anyhow, I would never have met Francine had I not stayed in that ratty old dorm…another horrible mistake! She was Carmela's best friend!

The fire boss at the mine where I was working, Igor "The Enforcer" Gunderson, just happened to be Francine's old man. I remember him well…the son-of-a-bitch. He was built like a brick toilet and no one messed with this guy. One day he invited me to his rat-infested hole in the wall office. It was full of coal dust and all kinds of shit. He said he had an important message to deliver. It was important alright!

"Listen to me, fuckhead!" he said. His gruff intimidating voice could have scared the jewels off a sperm whale. I mean, this dude was beyond terrifying. He walked with his fists clenched, shoulders high, and his head down…kind of reminded people of a giant monkey… like King Kong, to tell you the truth.

He said, "If my daughter sheds one tear, hear me and hear me well, just one tear because of you, I want you to see what I'm gonna do to your fuckin' body. Follow me!" He led me to a section of the coal mine where there was an enormous contraption with an electric cutter that undercuts coal and drops it on a conveyer belt. It's fifteen feet high and has sharp teeth five feet long. I knew what he was talking about because I was assigned to work that part of the mine for a few days. It scared the crap out of me. Accidents happened there all the time.

"Picture your body parts on this conveyer belt rolling beside hunks of coal." He pointed to the middle of the conveyor belt. "One leg will be over there, at the beginning, but they will be so black, no one will even notice them. Your body will be ground up like a chili dog and your head will be one black chunk blending perfectly into the larger chunks of coal on the belt. After the cutting apparatus does its thing with you, there will be no 'you' anymore! So, now tell me you understand Festo or Festus or whatever the hell your goddamn name is."

I hesitated, not because I didn't know what to say, but because I was too petrified to talk. Without saliva, my mouth felt like dry gulch canyon.

"Yes." I finally said. "But I would never hurt your daughter. You have to believe me."

"That's what the last guy said, and his body parts are pushing up daffodils behind the coal mine. The cutter was dull, and he screamed quite a bit until his head was completely hacked off. I was a little worried about being reported, but the guys here…they would never dare to cross me!"

"Also, for your information, no matter where you go, I will always find you and bring you back here!"

After that experience, I decided life with Francine wasn't all that bad. We had a thing going on. We shacked up for a good six months. Until she caught me making out in her bed with Jessica. Francine was pissed, and I mean pissed! When she moved out and told Igor about Jessica, he came looking for me. I correctly assumed that her father's wrath was more harmful to my health than working in the coal mine, so I got the hell out of Dodge quickly and fled to the Adirondack Mountains where Igor would never find me, or so I thought.

But Francine found me drying out in a half-way house in Bridgetown. She rented an apartment and nursed me back to sobriety. At least I got her maniac old man off my ass. So, we lived together for about a year. Then she got pregnant! I wanted her to give up the baby! No such luck! Fuck! So now I have a 'squaw' and 'tyke' and I'm only twenty-two! But I deeply love my son Tyler – more than anyone else in the world.

Jeff's mind "switched gears" faster than he could downshift. He looked at the gas gauge. The Firebird was dry, and he needed another bottle of Labatt's Blue. He stopped at a mobile mart near Schenectady to fill both tanks.

As he approached Bridgetown, a broad smile crossed his face. He would see Tyler soon. It didn't matter to Jeff how rarely he visited Francine. She should understand that I am doing the man's part as the breadwinner and she should shut up and be grateful. After all, the only thing she had to worry about was Tyler. I really don't love her anyway. Back in Morgantown, she was a good lay and I was scared shitless of Igor, her old man. Now, most of the time, she's too pickled to pop. When alone with her, Jeff thought only about his tiny cabin hideaway on Schroon Lake and his eagerness to get back there to snag a few absent-minded Salmon. He couldn't help it. Fishing was part of his DNA.

After three hours on the road, he arrived in Bridgetown. He turned into a small dirt driveway adjacent to the railroad tracks on Market Street. He looked at the clock in the car. It was 4:30 pm. He grabbed the remaining brown paper bag from the trunk and walked up the outside stairs that appeared to be built with scrawny kindling wood from all the dead trees in the area. That stupid damn mayor! I told him straight up to clean up this place! Those bastards in the village sit on their asses while the town goes to hell in a hand basket!

When Jeff entered the apartment, Francine was sitting at the kitchen table nursing a cold cup of coffee with one hand and holding a half empty bottle of Southern Comfort with the other.

Same old horseshit, he thought.

"Hey honeybunch," he murmured awkwardly. "What's goin' on? Sorry…I really couldn't get away the last few weekends. We had to move a thirty-thousand-foot cable reel to another place. And, as usual I had to do all the work myself!"

"Oh, really," she said with a caustic tone. "You're such a lousy martyr!"

"Really, Franny. Most those guys ain't got no clue how to move cable. If I ever quit they'd be shit out of luck! The whole damn place would fold!"

"Now, that wouldn't be such a bad idea and you know what? I hope you fold with it!" She filled her coffee cup with Southern Comfort until it overflowed.

"And what makes you think I give a good goddamn, anyway?" Her eyes were full of tears with a look of hopelessness and despair.

Jeff opened the antiquated Amana fridge he picked up at a garage sale and looked inside. "Oh, I see you didn't get my Labatt's Blue this week like I told you to? That's what I drink all the time in the mountains."

"I'm ain't your slave. Get you own fuckin' beer!"

Pretending to ignore her unpleasant mood, he lit up a Marlboro, and attempted to change the subject. "Franny, you can't believe the small ashtray in my Firebird. By the time I got home there was 'standing room' only! I gotta stop with these damn coffin nails! They're gonna kill my ass someday."

She glared at him like an irate gladiator. "Like I said, what the hell makes you think I give a damn? Do me a big favor! Buy some goddamn life insurance and then smoke your ass to death!"

Francine's blue eyes were swollen dynamite red. Her uncombed blonde hair added to her frazzled appearance. She had potential and could be a very attractive young woman, that is, if she cared enough to take care of herself. Her hand shook uncontrollably as she slowly raised her coffee cup to her mouth.

"I despise you!" She screamed. "I'm doing all the work around here! You could come home every week if you really wanted to! So, just turn your ass around and go the hell back to the mountains where you belong. You don't care about Ty and me! I don't want you comin' 'round here anymore!"

"Franny, how could you be so pissed off? What the hell! I break my ass all week for you!" He took the brown paper bag, turned it upside down, and dumped a pile of hundred-dollar bills on to the table. "There! See how good I take care of you? You ain't never gotta worry about nothin'!"

"Okay! Bring it on! The more money, the better," she said as she collected the cash on the table as if she had just won a jackpot in Vegas. "That's really all you're good for anyway!"

Jeff stood in frozen shock. He felt rejected and demoralized. "You know how hard I gotta work for that money? How could you be so damn ungrateful?"

Alternating her crying with fits of high-pitched screams, Jeff never had seen her so distraught.

"Last week, on Ty's eighth birthday," she said, "He was so sick I had to take him to emergency. I thought he was going to die… his fever was so high!"

Her head was pitched to one side as she slumped lower in the chair. "You never answer your goddamn phone! I had to deal with the doctors and everybody by myself. The more stressed I got, the angrier I was getting. I decided right then and there this was the last straw. No more I said to myself. No more! I want a divorce and I never want to see you again!"

With his eyes ablaze, as if Satan himself had seized his soul, he picked up the bottle of Southern Comfort, wound up like Mariano Rivera, and was ready to slam it against the kitchen wall.

"Sure, go ahead," she coaxed, "lose your temper! You animal! Get out! I hate you!" She stormed out of the kitchen and went into the bedroom slamming the door behind her.

Jeff sat down at the kitchen table more than a little distressed. Despite the anger he felt, he realized he was wrong. One important thing about Jeff…the delineation between right and wrong was always clear to him even if his behavior was, most of the time, on the "flip side of right". He placed his head down and began massaging his forehead with his left hand. He took a swig from the bottle of Southern Comfort. It went down smoothly and seemed to placate his anger of the moment.

"Hi Daddy," came a voice from the hallway. "Why is Mommy so angry?"

"Hi Ty! How you doin' big guy?"

"Well okay, I guess. Why was Mommy crying and screaming?"

"Mommy is tired and not feeling very good."

"Daddy, are you gonna leave again? I don't want you to go. I hate it when you aren't here. I don't like it when Uncle Billy comes over and is always yelling at Mommy and me."

"Does he come here a lot, Ty?" Jeff asked.

"He comes over during the week and stays overnight. I just go to my room and mind my own business, but I can hear him yelling at Mommy."

The hair on the back of Jeff's head bristled and he squirmed in the chair as if he had red ants crawling in his underwear. "Can you hear what he is saying?"

"He keeps asking Mommy to let some guy come over. I don't know who the guy is, but Uncle Billy keeps yelling about it. It scares me very much, Daddy."

Jeff clenched his fists in anger until his knuckles hurt. Jeff and his brother, Billy, fought like rabid dogs all their lives. Each of them has their own distinct battle scars to show for it. To Jeff he was and always will be an adversary.

I want to be with you. Please Daddy? Can I move in with you? Can you take me back to the mountains with you?"

"We'll see, Ty…we'll see."

"You always say 'we'll see', Daddy. I know, when you say that, you really mean 'no'."

Jeff bent down and hugged Tyler. Both were sniffling and struggling to hold back their tears.

"I love you, Daddy."

"I love you too, Ty."

Later, Jeff managed to talk Francine out of a divorce and thus evade the inevitable ferocity of Igor the "Enforcer" as well as the "chili dog machine". Not surprisingly, Jeff continued his very generous financial support for Francine and Tyler. When he came home, he would pick Tyler up and go fishing in a nearby canal. Soon, Tyler shared Jeff's passion for fishing and couldn't wait for hid dad to show up on weekends.

But there were other serious problems. One day Tyler was found by a neighbor sitting by himself on the railroad tracks crying his eyes out. "I hate my mother!" he sobbed. "I don't want to live with her! I want my Daddy!"

When the neighbor tried to persuade him to come with her, he ran into the switchyards, where railroad cars are interchanged, and trains are assembled. Fortunately, a yard worker saw him and used a sounder beacon with a bright blinking red light to stop a cab switcher pulling a load of freight cars. It stopped only a few feet away from Tyler.

When the police finally retrieved him, they contacted Social Services. Francine was interviewed but was so thoroughly inebriated she didn't even remember Tyler's name. She was declared an unfit mother. After considerable tears and heartache, Tyler ended up in a foster home and Francine in a wellness center for some much-needed therapy. Jeff tried to get custody of Tyler, but Francine did a pretty good job of sabotaging his character. Jeff never forgave her for that.

When Francine was discharged from the wellness center, Uncle Billy was waiting for her at her apartment. "Stay the hell away from me!" she told him.

"You need me!" he exclaimed. He knew she was in desperate straits. "How you gonna survive…no job, no money, no nothing! I'll tell you what, Sweetie Pie… how 'bout if I move in? I'll take care of the groceries and rent and sleep in Tyler's room. After all, you are my sister-in-law, I mean, listen…we are family."

Maybe it was her loneliness during her time spent at a wellness center that made her so vulnerable or maybe she was just trying to get even with Jeff. Whatever the case, it was inconceivable to Jeff that Billy was now a permanent resident of his apartment. To say Jeff loathed him with a deep rage was an understatement. I refuse to have anything to do with that bastard! He really is a wild dog who should be shot! And…I just might be the one who pulls the trigger!

Jeff and Billy's relationship grew toxic five years earlier when they both lived at home with their elderly parents. Billy, burly as a grizzly bear and just as vicious, eclipsed Jeff's flagpole physique by at least a hundred pounds and had no problem bashing him whenever the opportunity arose. And, it arose often. One time, for no apparent reason, Billy threw Jeff down the cellar stairs causing multiple injuries. Jeff spent three days in the hospital and his mother begged him not to press charges against Billy to which Jeff, to pacify his mother, reluctantly agreed.

But as it turned out, there were more reasons for the venomous relationship between Billy and Jeff. After Francine was released from the wellness center, Billy immediately introduced her to cocaine and pimped her out for his own personal financial gain. He beat her mercilessly when she resisted. Tyler would rebel against Billy's treatment of her. Then the day came when Uncle Billy beat up Tyler and he was taken to the hospital. Francine called the police and Billy was incarcerated but only for a few days. That was not long enough to satisfy Francine, so she complained to Jeff.

When Jeff picked Tyler up for a weekend of fishing, and noticed the bruises on his face, it was like a stick of dynamite detonated in Jeff's brain. He immediately went looking for Billy and found him on a barstool at a local bar.

There were no words exchanged. It was a surprise attack. Jeff blind-sided him with a sucker punch knocking him off a barstool and then pouncing on him like an angry gorilla. Before Billy could respond, Jeff inflicted grave injuries: a concussion, broken jaw, and broken ribs. As Billy lie withering in pain on the floor, Jeff issued a stern ultimatum: "If you ever touch my son again, I will kill you."

Jeff struggled to control the deep hatefulness brewing inside of him, one that often manifested itself in severe temper tantrums over insignificant things. He was seeing someone he loved tortured and was unable to do anything about it. Eventually, Jeff became a moody and irritable person.

He liked to drink beer with Monroe Engle, a close friend in Bridgetown, and unload his feelings of frustration regarding Billy and Francine. Still, he would fly off the handle and go into a hysterical rage over things that were none of his business.

For instance, while sitting with Monroe one sunny afternoon drinking Labatt's Blue on his front porch, he grumbled about Francine and Billy along with other people in his life whom he believed "screwed" him. He spoke mostly about his son, Tyler, how much he loved him, and how exasperated he was without him. The more he drank the more incensed he became.

A young mother with a four-year-old child walked by them on the front sidewalk. The child was crying nonstop as the mother kept spanking her backside trying to make her stop. Suddenly, Jeff stormed off the porch. Running to the sidewalk, he got right in her face and shouted, "You fuckin' bitch! Who do you think you are hitting that kid!" The woman was petrified. She picked up her child and ran away screaming. Jeff went back to the porch and said to Monroe, "She should be sent to jail for slappin' her kid like that!"

"By the way, Jeff," Monroe said nervously, "she lives next door. And all I can say is you just made a horrible blunder." With that, Monroe walked into his house.

Just then, what looked like an NFL linebacker on steroids came running across the front lawn towards Jeff. He stood there preparing himself for battle but before he knew what hit him, he was on the floor with blood coming out of his left ear.

"How dare you call my wife a 'fuckin bitch'?" Then he kicked Jeff three times in the side. By the time Monroe returned, Jeff was leaning against the outer railing in excruciating pain heaving his guts out.

Monroe drove him to the emergency room at Highland Hospital. He was there for a few days with three broken ribs and a punctured ear drum. Jeff threatened to get even by burning the guy's house down. He eventually cooled off but never forgot what the guy did to him. Nor did the guy ever forget about Jeff. He told Monroe next time he saw Jeff, "he would really beat the shit out of him and finish the job!"

CHAPTER SEVEN

Romano Sandpits, Bridgetown–July 1995

The condensation forming on the windows of the customized Chevy Van obscured the view of anything else in the forest that night. Even if the windows were clear, Tommy Desmond and Judy Flynn, two recent college graduates, as entwined as they were with each other, would never have noticed the man hiding in the bushes on the other side of a knoll about thirty feet from the van.

The mattress in the back of the van made love making easy. They could both stretch out but getting each other's clothes off was the bigger challenge.

"You can take them off now," she said softly.

As he pulled down her tight jeans, she arched her back making it easier. Then she unbuttoned and unzipped his Levi shorts. He always marveled at her beautiful body, her long legs, her mesmerizing blue eyes. He couldn't wait for the day they were married so he could have sex with her every night.

"I have to roll over," he said. "It's the only way I can get them off."

"Don't move," she said. "I can slide them off."

After she removed his shorts, she removed her bra and panties and he got rid of his underwear by flinging them like a sling shot to the front of the van.

She seemed uncomfortable. "Is there something wrong?" he asked.

"I don't know, she said. I keep hearing noises. I just feel so helpless totally undressed in the back of some van."

"Well then, let's have at it," he smiles impatiently.

She positioned her body on top of him. He could feel the sweet ecstasy as she bore down on him. "I love you," he whispered.

"I love you too," she responded as she leaned forward to kiss him.

Just then the rear butterfly doors of the van flew open. Before they could react, a man with a pistol grabbed her with one arm and, at the same time, pistol whipped Tom into a state of unconsciousness. Judy screamed and tried to fight back, but he pinned her arms to the mattress. Then proceeded to violently rape her until she passed out.

An hour later Tom opened his eyes. At first, he was delirious and disoriented. He saw Judy motionless and sobbing in the corner of the van with her knees up. He moved beside her and held her in his arms. Her lip was bleeding, and she had black and blue marks all over her body. They were both crying.

"I feel so dirty," she sobbed.

"Let's get the hell out of here before he comes back!"

Tom got behind the wheel of the van and noticed the keys were gone. "I left them in the ignition." he said. "That bastard took them!"

As he wiped off the condensation from the inside of the front windshield, an obnoxious, vile, and sickening face with a big sinister smile appeared glued against the windshield. For a moment, Tommy was frozen in fear. He darted to the rear of the van and tied a rope around the back-door handles, then ran over to comfort Judy.

"Hang in there, Sweetheart, I'll get us the hell out of here!" She was shaking so much he thought perhaps she wouldn't make it. He was getting desperate. Maybe I can hotwire this thing, he thought. He bounded back to the driver's seat, reached under the dash behind the ignition and found the wires he was looking for. He yanked them out and touched them together. The van started. He placed the transmission shift in drive and floored the accelerator.

The face, still on the windshield, looked hideous. He slammed on the brakes to jerk it off. It was still there. His hands trembled as he gripped the steering wheel.

"Get the fuck off, you lousy bastard!" he screamed. He headed down a dirt road and when he made the sharp right turn onto Commercial Street, he could see the face slowly slide off the van. Finally! he thought. Now to the hospital!

The next day, Chief of Police Lefty Margolis was surprised by a visit from Michael when he returned to Bridgetown from Schroon Lake. He wanted Lefty to place an ATL (attempt to locate) order for Jeff not only for Bridgetown but for the entire county. At first, he resisted. Lefty was well-aware of Jeff's peculiarities. He had several unfavorable clashes with him over the years. Truth be known, he couldn't care less about finding him. Finally, after a persuasive argument from Michael, he reluctantly agreed to put in the ATL.

Lefty was a large unusual man of sixty years old. His nickname originated from his days as one of the best left-handed softball pitchers in the area. He pitched 61 no-hitters and 9 perfect games and won several championships. Since those hallowed days on the mound, he had gained at least 100 pounds and now tipped the scales at 290. Michael could see the folds of his stomach crunched into the desk he was sitting behind. He had tight curly hair that was as white as his skin. The coke bottle lenses in his gray framed glasses blurred his big blue eyes. An ever-present slimy unlit cigar draped from his mouth and as disgusting as it was, most townsfolk wouldn't be able to recognize him without it.

He employed two full-time deputies, Thomas Prescott and Ralph Williams. They have been with the Bridgetown Police Department for about a month. Lefty fired the last two deputies for insubordination.

Turnover has always plagued the department. Part of the reason was low pay. But Lefty's dictatorial leadership style, enormous ego, lack of training, and obsessive allocation of work, played a major role in their departure.

"I'm convinced Jeff's receiving some kind of personal assistance," Michael told the chief. "In his condition, he could never escape from the hospital and he sure as hell couldn't be navigating out there on his own for this long."

"Just give me the facts, Lad. I'll draw my own conclusions. I have been chief for thirty-five years now, you know. I'm pretty good at what I do!" Michael noticed the four gold bars embroidered into the shoulders of his dark blue shirt and the large shiny gold badge on his left shirt pocket that said Chief on top and Bridgetown Police on the bottom. Lefty was single and had nothing better to do than over-manage police officers and under-deliver police services.

"So, who's the other oddball we are looking for?" Lefty asked, as he slithered the cigar from side to side in his mouth. Michael marveled at the chief's ability to chew an unlit cigar and talk at the same time.

"Good question," Michael replied. Then he proceeded to disclose the entire Schroon Lake saga to the chief. As Michael was telling the story, Lefty shook his head in shocked disbelief.

"Fucking amazing!" Lefty said with a frozen stare. "Well, why not let the pain in the ass die if he doesn't want to be found? I'm in the business of finding criminals, not some idiot who escaped from a hospital and is hiding somewhere like a frightened raccoon. "Did he commit a crime?"

"He's harmless. You know that!"

"Hmm… I don't know that. How would I? We're always finding new 'crazies' around town. You probably heard what happened yesterday up at the Romano Sand Pits. Someone scared the bejesus out of a college dude who was trying to get laid in his Chevy Van. Some deranged asshole gave him one helluva pistol whoppin' up there. Then he beat the crap out of his girlfriend and raped her. She's hurt badly and still in the hospital. Her boyfriend…he ain't in very good shape either."

Michael remembered Jeff's stories about when he was a young boy and his older brother, Billy would give him a hard time at home. Jeff would escape to the "pits' and hide out.

"The sandpits, you know," Lefty said, "are on the east side of Bridgetown next to a large forest. Parts of the forest were excavated by the Romano Construction Company creating large pits of sand used for mixing cement for construction purposes. They got excavation equipment up there now and are gonna start tearing through big hunks of land.

"Kids used to go up there and have BB-gun fights and shoot squirrels," Michael said.

"Not too bright but I remember… the goddamn kids. They still do it! Mark my words…sooner or later some kid's gonna lose an eye or worse!"

"That's a shame about those people that got beat up." Michael lamented. "Maybe you should check with the construction company for any suspicious employees."

"Listen, Michael! I don't need no one telling me how to do my job!"

"Sorry. Just trying to help, Chief. Tell me, do you think Jeff could be hiding up there?" Michael asked.

"Could very well be," Lefty said. "Now, that I think about it, maybe him and that fat ass screwball friend of his had something to do with the attack."

"C'mon, Lefty…you know Jeff better than that. He would never do such a thing."

"And, by the way, 'never' is a word I never use in law enforcement. There are way too damn many surprises…not that I'm ever proven wrong, mind you. In my thirty-five years on the force, believe me, I know what the hell I'm talking about! Everyone's a suspect, then again, no one's a suspect."

"I don't know about his lunatic brother, Billy, though," Lefty continued. "That guy freaks me out! He's a loner and never says jack shit to anybody and he wears those goddamn heavy flannel shirts all summer long. But I got to tell you, Billy is about as flaky as they come. And there ain't nobody home upstairs in his noodle either. You never know. I'm sending a couple of deputies up to the pits to track down that fanatic who raped that poor girl…assuming he's still there. Who knows? Maybe it will turn out to be Jeff or that Godzilla freak he's with. Maybe it will be Billy. Maybe it will be Frankenstein. Who the fuck knows?"

"Listen to me, Lefty!" Michael pleaded. "Jeff is in such excruciating pain he could never rape anyone! Even if he were healthy, he would never do such a thing. Believe me! I know him well. Also, because of his pain he's probably ornery as the devil. I don't want some trigger-happy deputy to shoot first and ask questions later. Know what I am saying, Lefty?"

"Okay…enough already! I've had about enough of law enforcement 101. Look…you're not telling me anything I don't know. He has a temper too! I know that! So, what? If he gives us a hard time, he'll go right into the hoosegow!"

"Oh, one more thing…" Michael said, "I think he has a gun."

"Goddamn it! And exactly when were you going to get around to telling me that, after he put a bullet in my head? So, who was the idiot that gave him a gun?"

"Well, Lefty, you signed off on his pistol permit…remember?"

Michael walked out of the chief's office thoroughly disgusted. He knew the deputies were about as worthless as the Chief. If they went to the pits and startled Jeff, he might react like wounded animal and start shooting. Then they would kill him for sure. But then again, why would I worry about that? No way Jeff is up there anyway. Maybe I should go up there and check for myself. On second thought, I'll let the Bridgetown deputies mess it up.

Chapter Eight

July 1993 – Bridgetown–Wayne and Molly Winslow

Wayne Winslow, Bridgetown High's athletic director, and Molly, his devoted spouse, were exceptional citizens of Bridgetown. Both were very much involved with Bridgetown youth and various civic organizations and were among the most respected people in the community.

One evening, a few years ago, while driving home from an evening baseball game, Wayne Winslow was perplexed by his wife Molly's silence and asked, "Sweetheart, you have been very quiet all evening. Is something wrong?"

"I'll be fine," she replied. "It's just that every time I go to a high school game, I get a little down seeing all the kids and their parents. It reminds me of how badly I want children." Then she began to cry.

"We'll have children, Sweetheart. We just need to keep trying." Wayne's words had little effect. Molly's desire for children were deep and as much as he attempted to console her, he knew the only way to ease her pain was to have a child.

"I cannot get through life without having children!" Molly said. "Ever since I was a young girl, becoming a mom was the main goal in my life. I mean… I had other goals too like going to college. I took forever to select a major. Maybe it was a lack of commitment but all I really wanted to do was graduate, get married, and have a flock of kids. I had six siblings and we did everything together. So, a large family was a forgone conclusion…at least for me it was."

But after years of trying and many exhausting physical examinations, it was determined that Molly had endometriosis. They tried fertility treatments for at least a year but complications, including pelvic pain, made it difficult for Molly to cope with everyday activities.

Neither Wayne nor Molly were prepared for the financial, physical, and psychological struggles associated with her treatments.

"All our credit cards are maxed out," Wayne complained. "I don't know how much longer I can afford these fertility treatments. Most of our medical claims have been denied. Paying for these tests out of pocket is damn expensive!"

When the doctors discovered pelvic cysts and told Wayne and Molly they could rupture and cause blockages in the gastrointestinal tracts, they became alarmed.

"It's just not fair!" Molly declared. "Two people who love children as much as we do…and can provide a wonderful home for them…and we can't have any."

"I've had enough!" Molly cried after a particularly long and painful treatment day. They met with a doctor who advised against further treatments.

Molly persisted, "Wayne, I think we should adopt an infant. When a newborn child is adopted, it is almost like it is your own biological child. What do you think?"

So, Wayne researched the chances of an infant adoption and discovered it was so much more difficult and complicated than he thought.

"Molly, roughly ten percent of hopeful parents get a baby. The wait is often long and full of disappointment and heartbreak. Legal fees are astronomical. Listen, Sweetheart, after the costs of fertility treatments, we need time to recover financially. My teaching and coaching salary just about gets us through the month. I'm sorry Molly, it's very frustrating, I know."

Molly's personal self-esteem began to erode, and she plunged into a state of deep depression until one day when Wayne came home and found Molly in the bathroom with an open bottle of benzodiazepine on the counter, a medication her doctor gave her for anxiety relief and to allow her to sleep at night.

"Molly! How many of these did you take?" he asked her, as he flushed the remaining pills in the bottle down the toilet.

"Only a few," she mumbled dazed and confused. Fortunately, Wayne got to her soon enough to avoid a hospital visit.

"Listen to me!" he asserted. "I can't bear the thought of losing you, Molly! Our life together is too damn precious. If we never have children, we still have each other. You must remember that and never try anything like this again! Promise me!"

"I'm sorry. I had a weak moment after talking to the doctor. It won't happen again. I promise."

Wayne shook his head as he starred intensely at Molly, clearly infuriated that she would even think of committing suicide. "I know this have been very difficult for you, but we have to get through this together."

"I know, Sweetheart. I know," she said.

Suddenly, Wayne became severely distraught and on the verge of panic. His insides were rumbling. He jumped up, ran to the kitchen, and vomited. The thought of losing Molly was overwhelming and he was completely unprepared to deal with it. Then he started to cry relentlessly.

Later, he found Molly in the bedroom curled up on the bed. She was also in tears.

"I'm so sorry, Sweetheart!" she said as they embraced. Wayne wiped her eyes then wiped his own. They held each other silently for a long time until Wayne unlocked the embrace and slowly pulled away.

"I think we should investigate the possibility of a foster child." he said. "What do you think, Sweetheart? Can't hurt to consider it, right?"

Molly hesitated a few moments, put her head down and reached for Wayne's hand.

"I'm so scared," she sobbed.

"I know, Sweetheart. I am too. Michael Alexander talked to me the other day about the possibility of foster parenting. He knew we were trying to adopt without success. He told me about foster parenting classes being offered over at the community college. Is it okay with you if I check into these classes?"

Molly dithered a bit. She looked away from Wayne and shrugged her shoulders as if she viewed having a foster child was some sort of consolation prize. "Oh, I don't know. Let's get more information then we can discuss it."

"Of course," Wayne replied.

Molly finally decided she wanted to learn more, and they enrolled the following semester. The first thing they learned was that the overriding goal of foster parenthood was for the child to return home. The primary reason to remove a foster child was the threat of imminent danger whether it was physical, sexual, or neglect. But before a child can return home, families must prove that their home is safe for children to return.

"What if we get attached?" Molly asked.

"In most cases, you will get attached," the teacher replied. "How could you not?"

Good foster parents always emphasize to the children that they will be loved no matter where they live."

"I have a hard time with that," Molly said. "You love and care for a child as if he or she is you own and suddenly they are whisked away and sent back to their parents."

"I understand," the teacher said. "This is a hurdle all foster parents need to get over. The child will eventually leave you and honestly, if you cannot accept that, then perhaps you should not be a foster parent."

Wayne and Mary finished the course, received their graduation certificates, and began working with an agency to locate a foster child. Knowing the situation with Tyler Walden, Michael referred him to the social services and the agency. After a few months, many interviews, lots of soul searching, Tyler was placed with Wayne and Molly.

Chapter Nine

July 1995–Bridgetown

Michael was euphoric. Being designated as one of the Top 100 Financial Advisors in the country by Fortune Magazine, had provided him with a deep sense of career fulfillment. He kept saying to himself, I don't believe it! There are thousands of financial services representatives in the county and I was selected to be in the Top 100? It was almost as if he felt unworthy of the award.

It turns out Fortune Magazine solicited candidates for the award from the top financial services firm in the county. Ten clients with the largest number of assets under management from each company were interviewed for each candidate.

Michael had heard about the award from a few of his clients who were already congratulating him as if his selection was inevitable. While he appreciated the vote of confidence, never in a million years did he think he would even be a candidate let alone win the award.

With his wife, Megan and their two children, Jason and Teddy present, the award was presented to Michael during a black-tie ceremony at the Waldorf Astoria in New York City. He received a beautiful plaque engraved as follows:

We, the selection committee of Fortune Magazine hereby name Michael Alexander, CFP, as one of Fortune Magazine's Elite 100 Financial Advisors. Mr. Alexander has committed himself to placing the client's interest ahead of his own at all times when providing financial advice. Furthermore, said designee has acted with honesty, integrity, competence, and diligence.

Michael was exceedingly proud to receive this award. The Bridgetown Herald, the local newspaper, did a special piece on him and the Rotary Club, of which he was a long-standing member, honored him with a special banquet. Friends, clients, and colleagues extended their well-wishes.

He was especially pleased that he could "brag" about the award to his parents, whom he believed still held out hope that someday he would go to law school and join the ranks of other "Alexanders" with the barrister marque. Nevertheless, he could tell by their behavior, if not their words, they were really very proud of him.

Ample evidence existed that Michael had "arrived". He drove a top of the line BMW, his properties on Schroon Lake and Bridgetown were priceless, he was one of the most well-known supporters of community charitable events and a huge benefactor to the local Children's Hospital.

Michael returned to his office excited and confident as ever. After affixing the plaque to a prominent location inside his office, he had his secretary double his appointment goal for each week. Then he began researching his client accounts to determine if he could be of further assistance to them.

Later in the day, Francine made a rare call to Michael's office and asked that he stop by to discuss something very important. At first, he was reluctant but then thought maybe she had some information that would lead to Jeff's whereabouts. After his discussion with the chief, Michael felt badly that he hadn't pursued Jeff's disappearance further. Jeff would materialize when he was good and ready. However, there were days when Michael felt particularly remiss for not having been more persistent.

He arrived at Francine's apartment later in the afternoon on his way home from work. When he entered the front door, he was surprised by a woman who looked completely different. Strikingly beautiful with soft blonde hair, dark eyelashes, and a tall curvaceous figure, he never realized just how pretty Francine was. Most of the time, when he saw her around town, she was disheveled and tousled looking… like she just got out of bed… and if the truth be told, she probably did.

"Congratulations on your selection, Michael! It's a great honor for you as well as for Bridgetown."

"I'm making Beef Stroganoff. It's good with strips of beef and the creamy sauce I use. I also put mushrooms and tomatoes in it. It's my father's favorite." Michael remembered the story Jeff told him about Francine's father, Igor, the fire boss at the West Virginia coal mine and how he threatened to carve up Jeff in the coal cutting device if anything ever happened to Francine.

"By the way, how is your father?"

"Nasty as ever," Francine replied. "He's coming up next week to visit me. I'm sure his mere presence here will shake up Bridgetown. Michael, if he ever finds out about Billy beating me up, I seriously fear for Billy's life."

"Then again," Michael smirked, "Maybe he would be doing the world one big goddamn favor!"

Francine smiled and nodded. "Yeah, I would be happy to provide the gun!"

"Michael, can you stay for dinner? I think you will enjoy my father's recipe."

"Thanks, I don't mean to be rude, but I can't." He looked down at his watch. "Megan probably has dinner already on the stove."

Michael realized that if Megan ever discovered that he had dinner with Francine, a cataclysmic event like an Indian Ocean Tsunami would surely erupt. He really couldn't afford to have his marriage disrupted by the town hooker.

"Sorry, I didn't mean to put you in an uncomfortable position. I just need someone to help me. I'm asking you to stay because I know how close you are to Jeff and Tyler and I thought maybe we could discuss some things over dinner."

She broke down and started to cry. "I've really ruined my life and now I'm trying to figure out a way to make up for it. I've been sober for four months. It's so hard! I finally got a restraining order against Billy. If he ever shows up here again, I'll have the bastard arrested."

Michael hesitated for a moment wondering what to say. He admired people who were trying to overcome personal weaknesses. But he knew how many times she had tried and failed before. Also, he felt awkward with Francine because of his good relationship with Wayne and Molly, Tyler's foster parents. After all, he was the one who helped them acquire custody of Tyler.

"Okay," he conceded. "How can I assist, Francine?"

"I want my son back," she said bluntly. "He's my son and deserves to be with me!"

"What about Jeff?" Michael asked. "Do you want him back too?"

"I have to think long and hard about that one."

"You do realize that Tyler is embarrassed and very angry over your behavior."

He paused a minute waiting for her reaction.

"I know," she said. "And how could I possibly blame him?"

"He gets bullied all the time in high school because of it, through no fault of his own. He's a good kid with a kind heart and he works hard on his studies. He always hated Billy. Tell me…why is Billy not in jail…after all the physical abuse he has inflicted upon you and Tyler?"

"My God! Do you know how many times I have been beat up by that bastard? I don't think my ribs are ever going to heal. He's controlled every part of my life! No…I never called the police. How could I involve them? He was paying for everything… the rent, the groceries. I was too messed up to get a job, so he had me right under his thumb. Now, after all that time in the wellness center under a doctor's supervision, I feel stronger and more determined to help myself. I have a new job at Skip's Bakery and I'm earning my own money and I'm really determined to change my life."

"That's wonderful, Francine. I really admire you for trying so hard." Michael felt compassion for Francine. She really wasn't a bad person. But she was very sick. She tried but could never overcome her weaknesses. Maybe this time will be different, he thought. Maybe this time, with Billy out of the picture, she had a fighting chance.

She put the place mats on the table. "You will stay, right?"

Michael tossed it around in his head for a few moments. Somehow, he felt compelled to help Francine, yet he didn't know how.

"I need to leave early," he said. At that moment, he realized his fate was sealed and the wrath of Megan would be upon him no matter what time he arrived home. It was unavoidable. He would have to tell her the truth. He always believed the truth was the cornerstone of their marriage.

Michael took off his suit coat and tie and placed them over one of the living room chairs.

"How can I help?" he asked.

"You just relax. I'll turn on TV and you can watch CNN. The Stroganoff will be ready in just a few minutes."

"I prefer Fox News," he said with a smile.

"Okay. Would you like a drink?"

"Sure. Would love a Manhattan."

Francine made a perfect one for Michael and poured herself a Diet Coke. She placed the dishes and silverware on the table with care impressing Michael with her attentiveness. Then she lit two white candles in the center of the table.

They enjoyed a relaxing dinner together. Michael was impressed. Francine was charming, intelligent, and an excellent conversationalist. Not at all the woman he thought she was. Michael was surprised how contented he felt with her.

"I'm hoping to go to night school and get a degree," she said.

"What would you like to do? I mean, you know, what kind of career are you going to pursue?"

"Is it difficult to get into the financial planning business?" she asked.

"A degree in finance would certainly help. The next step would be to hook up with a financial planner who needs some help servicing his clients. An apprenticeship for a few years would be terrific...if you could find one. You learn the business and at the same time be of assistance to the planner…a win-win for both."

"What about you. Michael? Could I get an apprenticeship with you?"

Michael saw that question coming and was prepared for an answer. He realized hiring her now would be bad for business, but he liked the way she was thinking.

"I'll be honest with you, Francine. I think your willingness to change the direction of your life is marvelous. Really. You deserve much credit. Especially since you have managed to remove Billy from your life. But bringing you into my practice now would alienate several of my clients. I'll tell you what. For the lack of a better way to say it, if you continue the straight and narrow, get enrolled in an evening curriculum at the university with a major in finance, keep your job at the bakery… maybe we can do something next year. In fact, I'll even do this: I'll reimburse you for half of your tuition expense at the end of the first year as long as you receive passing grades."

Francine was taken aback. She knew Michael was one of the most trusted businessmen in Bridgetown. She reached across the table for Michael's hand. "You'd do that for me?" No one's ever done anything like that for me, ever!"

"Yes," he said. "But the burden of success is on you, Francine. You are the one who's going to make all the effort!" Michael downed the entire Manhattan. "You make a mean Manhattan," he said. She got up and made him another.

"Thank you," he said, as she gently placed a fresh Manhattan in front of him.

"So, what do you think of my proposition? Ah, whoops, I didn't mean to use that word."

Francine smiled. "No problem, Michael. Unfortunately, I do understand that language." Her self-effacing attitude scored more points with Michael.

"So, are we in agreement?" he asked.

"Oh, my God, yes!"

"Okay, I'll draw up an informal written agreement we can both sign when I get to my office tomorrow."

"It is so wonderful of you to do this for me. How can I pay you back?"

"Make me another Manhattan?" he quipped. "No, really, Francine don't worry about payback…just get your life in order. You are a smart woman. And now you have an opportunity to turn your life around. I hope you see it that way."

"Yes, definitely!" Francine rose from her chair at the table, made another Manhattan for Michael, and came around the table to sit closer to him. A part of Michael's brain told him to get up and get the hell out of Francine's apartment. Another part of his brain told him to stay.

Then she changed the subject. "Michael, do you think there is any way I can regain custody of Tyler? I need my son back."

"Well, you certainly have a big advantage. You are his mother. But under the circumstances the court will ask you to prove yourself competent. I can't tell you all the legalities…that's the job of a lawyer. Do you have one?" Michael took a big sip from his third Manhattan.

"No, can you help me find a good one?"

Michael immediately understood how difficult, if not impossible, it would be to find a lawyer in Bridgetown to represent her. Partly, because of her reputation but mainly because Tyler was living with Wayne and Molly Winslow, two upstanding members of the Bridgetown community, and they adored him.

"You must demonstrate your fitness to be his mother, not just talk a good game. Work on our agreement first, get in school, work hard, and as my father used to say, keep you skirts clean. Then after you succeed with that, you can try for custody. Does that make sense?" Alcohol was providing additional steam for Michael to say what he really meant.

"I don't want to wait that long! He's my child!"

"Allow me to ask you again. Would you ever consider a reconciliation with Jeff if it meant getting Tyler back? That's assuming we'd ever find him."

"My wounds are still fresh but maybe. He's in the woods someplace…probably up at Schroon Lake. That's his paradise!" It was clear to Michael that Francine had some underlying resentfulness.

"I really have to leave," Michael said, as he stood up and swayed side to side. "I'm afraid I'm starting to feel the effects of those Manhattans. Megan will be on the warpath when I get home. I feel so lightheaded." Michael wasn't sure whether it was Francine's sex appeal or the Manhattans, but one thing was for sure; he really did not want to go home.

"Michael, you can't drive home in your condition. Why don't you lie down for a few minutes and I'll make some coffee?" Francine led Michael to her bedroom. He was in no condition to resist, even if he wanted to.

"I can't believe I'm so queasy. A few Manhattans never had this kind of effect on me before."

"Just lie down here for a while." She puffed up the pillow behind his head and returned to the kitchen to make coffee.

Michael fell quickly into a deep slumber that lasted nearly three hours. It was 1:00 am when he opened his eyes. Everything was pitch black and he was totally disoriented and in a mental fog, aware only of the heavy breathing of someone beside him. He rolled over, reached out, and felt a warm, smooth and silky skin.

"Megan", he murmured. "I want you…move closer, Honey."

As her breathing became intense, her body erupted into several spasmodic surges. She was all over him. Suddenly, he needed and wanted her with a desire he hadn't felt in years. Her warm firm breasts pressed against him, her thighs wrapped around his waist. Then she started passionately caressing and kissing every part of his body. He had no control and for the moment, didn't want any. He desperately wanted her. She moved on top of him and for the next hour he had a sexual encounter like he had never experienced before. She was tantalizing and seductive and he just wanted more and more.

When Michael awoke at 8:00 a.m., still in a semi-inebriated state. When he saw Francine's naked body beside him, he flew out of bed quicker than a weasel with his tail on fire.

"Francine!" he hollered, "Christ sake! It was you!"

"Wasn't it wonderful?" she sighed. "C'mon, Michael, get back in bed with me." She was smiling tempestuously, irresistibly. Michael felt defenseless.

He looked at his watch. "Damn!" He asked himself, how the hell am I going to explain this to Megan? In fact, how the hell do I explain this to myself?

"C'mon Michael," Francine beckoned him again. When she sat up in the bed and let the sheet drop, Michael had no problem answering her call. They made passionate love for the next few hours. And when it was over, Michael knew that he had fallen in love with her.

This can't be possible. One go around in the sack and I'm in love? It was like a powerful surge of affection had invaded his heart. I've never felt like this before. I'm not supposed to feel like this! It's not right! It didn't take much more pondering for Michael to accept his feelings. The big question was, what was he going to do about it?

CHAPTER TEN

September 1995 – Bridgetown–Tyler Walden

Tyler Walden rarely misbehaved. In fact, all he really wanted to do was concentrate on his school work, participate in athletics and, once in a while, go fishing with his dad. Subjects relating to earth science, environmental pollution, and climate change were his primary interests. He had a passion for wildlife and the outdoors which he undoubtedly inherited from his father.

Yet, the relentless bullying he experienced at school bothered him. Teachers and students alike were well-aware of his mother's reprehensible lifestyle and his peers showed no mercy. Every opportunity to ridicule Tyler was exploited. Except for athletics, he avoided extracurricular activities. He hated drama and conflict. When backed into a corner, he would acquiesce and go through a process of self-incrimination that would last for days if not weeks.

Wayne, on the other hand, was the disciplinarian in the family and clashed with Tyler over his strict non-negotiable expectations. As the head coach of the football team, his frustration was most apparent on the football field, especially when Tyler made a mistake. If he dropped a pass or missed a block, Wayne would scold Tyler in front of the players. One could argue that Wayne was only trying to build Tyler's skills and make him a better athlete. One could also argue that it had more to do with Wayne's ego and his need for personal fulfillment at Tyler's expense.

Nevertheless, Wayne hated what Billy and Francine did to Tyler; the example they set, and the emotional distress it caused Tyler he believed could never be repaired. He was angered by what he considered Francine's complete lack of sensitivity with regard to Tyler and the nightmarish bullying her immorality caused him.

When kids ganged up on him and derided him, Tyler ignored them and refused to initiate a physical confrontation. Wayne simply could not understand why Tyler always backed down.

One day Tyler was walking out of the boys' locker room and three upperclassmen were waiting outside for him. "Just wondered if you could fix me up with your old lady?" John Flaherty asked. "I could satisfy her a lot better than all those drunks she sleeps with," he snickered. Flaherty wasn't a big kid but was smart enough to know Tyler wouldn't engage him no matter how many of his buttons he pushed. The two other boys stood there laughing and hoping to see a fight. Just then Wayne walked out the door and the boys scattered like frightened rabbits.

"Were those kids harassing you," he asked.

"Yeah, but I took care of it."

"You 'took care of it', huh? Tyler, what the hell is wrong with you? If it were me I'd kick their asses! You're a big guy! If you ever went after one of them, they'd all run for cover so fast it would make your head spin! The best way to stop that crap is to retaliate!"

"Retaliate?" Tyler asked with astonishment "You mean start a fight?" Tyler shook his head. "I am not a fighter."

"Yes! Damn it! Start a fight as a matter of principle!"

Tyler lowered his head. He thought for a moment and tried to choose the right words. He hated to disappoint Wayne. "I save my fighting for the football field," Tyler said. "I'm not comfortable beating kids up."

"Well, sometimes you just have to step up!"

"I am getting help from a counselor at school. His name is Dr. Kazuya. He told me 'the view from the high road always looks better.' He told me to walk away…unless someone got physical with me… I have a right to defend myself. I like Dr. Kazuya. I feel better when I talk to him. You know what else he said?" Tyler hesitated somewhat cautious about contradicting Wayne.

"Go ahead, Ty. Tell me what else he said."

"He told me it takes more courage to ignore them, than to fight them. He talked to me about 'dignified indifference' – the ability to rise above the fray. He said that bullying can teach us life lessons and instill strength and discipline. And, being a target of bullying can teach me how to manage disputes and interact with others.

"Oh, really. Well, I think that's a lot of BS! So, tell me, what else did Dr. Kazuya say, Tyler?"

"Hmm…. I don't think I should share everything he said. But it was terrible what happened to his mother and father." Tyler maintained close eye contact with Wayne and shifted around in his chair.

"One day he took me out to lunch and told me all about his family and the problems he had growing up during World War II. I think he was trying to help me deal with bullying."

"He used to travel between Harbin, China and Tokyo with his father who was a doctor and treated POWS. Then his father was killed when he refused to work on a plan to spread plague fleas along the west coast of the US. It was called Operation Cherry Blossoms at Night. Did you ever hear of it?

"No," Wayne answered, "but I knew the Japanese were in the process of developing germ warfare. Fortunately, the war was over before any of it could be implemented. Thousands of people would have been killed. I know that much."

"I felt really sorry for Dr. Kazuya." Tyler grimaced as his eyes filled with tears.

"How come, Tyler?"

"He said, 'My mom…she was forced into sexual slavery by the Japanese military after my dad was executed. Ten years old! That's how old I was when my mom was gang raped right in front of me. I can't begin to describe what they did to her. I turned into a vicious animal – losing all control – all I wanted to do was kill them all!'"

"He told you all that?"

"Yes. He even said…"

"Go ahead, Ty. What did he say?"

"'After it was over, and she was lying on the ground, I covered her with a blanket. She was shivering and bleeding all over and was in extreme shock – her pulse was weak, and her breathing was shallow – I couldn't bear to see her suffer. So, I gently placed the blanket over her face until she stopped breathing altogether.'"

"So, he killed her?"

Tyler nodded as his eyes were filled with tears. "He just helped her to… stop breathing."

"Stop breathing? So, it was a mercy killing?"

"I guess so…"

"So, what happened to Dr. Kazuya?" Wayne asked.

Tyler took a deep breath, looked away, then focused his eyes intently on Wayne.

"He was forced to be a male prostitute."

"How repulsive!"

"That's for sure! He said he very nearly committed suicide because of the shame he felt."

"I am somewhat surprised he didn't," Wayne noted. "They call it honor suicide and people in some countries do it to protect or restore their honor, especially after doing something shameful or bringing dishonor to their family."

"I just think he had lots of trouble dealing with the embarrassment."

"Living with himself must still be tough."

"There were several other children in the camp," Tyler continued, "I'm sure they must have been children from other women in the prison camp who were also prostitutes. But for some reason, he said, he was singled out and was bullied by the soldiers… probably because his mother and father resisted so much. He wouldn't tell me what they did to him. He said it was simply too humiliating.

"'They can call you names,' he said. 'And they can torture your body, but they cannot control your mind.' Through all the bullying and torture, he only thought about what he would do after he was released. So, then he said to me…'when I discuss bullying with you, I know what I am talking about! I've had years of experience with unspeakable bullying acts in a prison camp.'"

"How could I feel sorry for myself after hearing Dr. Kazuya's story? When I said that to him he said, 'I am so sorry it has hurt you so much, especially when they attack and make fun of your mom.'

I remember how upset up he got. It was almost like he was the one being bullied. 'It's very hard, he said, 'but you must walk away. If you throw a punch every time someone bullies you, you are no better than they are."

"Doesn't that make more sense than starting a fight, Wayne?"

"No! For crying out loud. Listen to me, Ty! Why don't you give me the names of the kids that bully you? I'll call them into my office and reprimand them and tell them to stop, or else there will be severe consequences."

"I don't want you or any other teacher to interfere. It's my problem and I will deal with it myself. I really have thought about it quite a bit. Dr. Kazuya has also given me some books to read. I'm going to build my social skills, think in a more positive manner, continue my sports programs along with meditation – like thinking through what is happening and learn how to respond in a more effective manner. I know I'm sometimes far-off and don't communicate like I should around the house. I will try harder. But I still feel my real mother and father have betrayed me. I can't help it but this makes me very angry. But I will always be grateful to you and Molly."

Wayne nodded slowly. His eyes were still teared up. Although Wayne would like to have challenged Tyler's answer, he realized that Tyler had seemed to have his head screwed on right. He was grateful for Dr. Kazuya's intercessions and advice. He finally stood up and said to himself, the kid sounds like he knows what he is talking about. But if it were me, I'd kick their bully asses so far down the street they'd be looking up from the sewer!

Chapter Eleven

September 1995–Bridgetown

Despite his somewhat inflexible attitudes about bullying, Wayne Winslow was a wonderful role model. He went to church every Sunday, didn't smoke or drink, taught a personal hygiene course at Bridgetown High and a Catechism class at St. Anthony's church. He was president of a self-help men's group that met monthly in the church gathering room. Above all, he was a principled person whose commitment to righteousness was unsurpassed. As coach of the Bridgetown Titans football team, he had led the team to five consecutive county championships. Football was a very big thing in Bridgetown. But coach Winslow really saw himself in the people development business. Seeing one of his players grow up to be a good citizen was his greatest joy.

Conversely, when a student flaunted his opportunities, it was extremely disturbing to the coach and he did have a temper.

The snow was piling up on the football field. Despite the best of efforts of the ground crew, the artificial turf was wet and icy. Coach Winslow ended his pre-game practice on a high note. He believed his Bridgetown Varsity Football Team was well-prepared for the big county championship game today with archrivals, the Belmont Blue Devils.

But Wayne wasn't your typical "rah-rah" coach and his players appreciated it because he conditioned them to appreciate it. Not that he wasn't enthusiastic and motivational, but his leadership had more depth than the typical high school football coach. For example, he didn't just dish out praise indiscriminately, rather he mastered the art of effective motivational management by distinguishing between exceptional performance and super exceptional performance.

Exceptional performance was expected. Effective blocking, tackling, pass catching, and running was "a player's job" and as such didn't deserve special recognition. Coach Winslow's worst nightmare was an overconfident football team; he believed a team that becomes complacent doesn't win football games. So, he refused to allow them to become comfortable with victory.

Tyler Walden flourished in this environment. As a freshman, he was already six feet tall weighing almost two-hundred pounds of pure muscle. His short golden hair and bulging biceps made young girls flock to him as if he was some sort of high school Adonis.

But his focus was on his studies and football, not on young girls. Although he was a "straight A" student, the teachers worried about his emotional adjustment. He was a loner. He had dreams of playing in the NFL like any other kid his age. Tyler really did have great potential. If not the NFL, certainly an athletic scholarship was in the offing. He realized without financial assistance, it would be impossible for him to attend college. He had to excel in the classroom and on the football field if he wanted to attend college and make a good life for himself.

No one worked harder to earn a starting position on the football team. By mid-season he was the starting wide receiver. But Tyler felt a great deal of stress today. He worried about making a dumb mistake that might cost Bridgetown the championship and letting the coach and fellow players down. If that happened, he simply wouldn't be able to live with himself.

Then again, he was always worrying. His mother, Francine, while she was on a path to recovery, was still known as the town hooker. His Uncle Billy, whom he despised with every fiber of his body, finally left the house. What a relief that was! He was always escorting men in and out of his mother's bedroom. Even at the young age of thirteen, Tyler knew what was going on and hated his uncle and his mother for it.

In school, Tyler tried to be anonymous. A daunting figure around school, most kids left him alone but behind his back he was known as the hooker's kid. When he heard someone making disparaging remarks, most of the time, he remained silent and walked away. It caused considerable shame and embarrassment for Tyler as it would for any adolescent student.

Yet, there were also things in Tyler's life for which he was grateful. Not only did he like playing football for Coach Winslow, about five years ago, the coach and his wife, Molly, were approved as his foster parents. Social Services found both Jeff and Francine unfit to raise Tyler. Jeff tried hard to secure custody but Francine bad mouthed him so badly, he didn't stand a chance. Michael interceded, knowing the Winslow's were fine upstanding members of the community who were already participating in foster parent training, he guided them through the New York State certification process for step parents.

There was a long period of adjustment. Wayne and Molly were persevering and had come to love Tyler. But Tyler longed to be with his father up in his Schroon Lake hideaway, fishing, and camping. But where was my father? He felt abandoned and was becoming very angry. Why didn't my dad at least contact me? he would ask himself over again. He knew about his father's accident at Schroon Lake and that he left the hospital in critical condition. Was he dead or alive? Tyler feared the worst and was emotionally obsessed with the whereabouts of his father. Every football game, he scanned the bleachers and the sidelines for any hint of his father.

Today, Michael and Megan were in the first row and were waving to him, cheering him on. Tyler waved back nervously and again the thought of making a game losing blunder crossed his mind.

Dr. Kazuya, his school counselor, managed to secure a spot on the bench. The previous week he offered his services to Coach Winslow. After all, he was a medical doctor too and was available free of charge for school athletic events.

Coach Winslow called his team together for a pre-game huddle and prayer.

They discarded their hoodie parkas and assembled around him on one knee. "Keep in mind what I told you guys!" he asserted. "No matter what the score ends up, remember one thing! Winning means going as far as you can with all that you've got. If you do that for the next forty-eight minutes, you will be winners! Now get out there and give it your all!"

After three-and-a-half quarters, Bridgetown was behind 18-7. The game was riddled with fumbles and interceptions. The cold wet weather was taking its toll on both teams. Belmont was getting ready to kick off after their last score. Both teams were in position.

"Tyler!" yelled the coach "Get in there and run that thing back to the end zone!" Tyler sprinted out to field and assumed his place to receive the kick off. He looked at the clock. The two-minute warning was coming up. This is my chance…I gotta do something with the ball, he said to himself.

It was a high arching kick. Tyler focused on the ball with laser like precision. Three opposing players were bearing down on him with malevolence in their eyes. His teammates screamed, "yell fair catch!" That way he could avoid getting tackled, fumbling or even getting hurt. Tyler wanted no part of it. He caught the ball and immediately slipped on the icy field. Then he got hit hard by two defenders fumbling the ball on the ten-yard line. As the ball bounced end over end toward the opponent's end zone, Tyler sprang to his feet, grabbed the ball, turned toward his own goal line and ran faster than a cheetah chasing a gazelle. No one was even close to him. As he crossed the goal line, the Bridgetown crowd went wild.

"My God!" Michael shouted, "I never knew that kid could run that fast!"

"He's on fire," Megan said. "Somehow the emotional setbacks in his life have been converted to physical energy. I think he's angry and football is an outlet."

"I'm not sure that's a good thing," Michael said. "Tyler is the type of kid that keeps everything inside. I wonder where he vents his anger when football is over?"

Megan looked at Michael and shrugged her shoulders. "He needs counseling," she said.

"What he really needs is his father," Michael countered.

Now the score was 18-14. The Bridgetown Titans needed another touchdown to win, and a three-point field goal was not enough. Expending their time outs, the Titans defense stopped the Blue Devils offense. Now, the Blue Devils were lining up to punt.

Coach Winslow huddled his team. "Tyler! This time, no matter what you want to do, I want you to yell 'fair catch' and leave it up to our offense to win this game! Do you understand?" demanded the coach.

"Yes, Sir," responded Tyler respectfully. He tightened the strap on his helmet and despite the coach's words, felt a compelling nearly irrepressible passion to win this game for Bridgetown.

Belmont's kick went deep into the end zone and ensured there would be no kick return. With less than minute to play, the Titan's, who were on the twenty-five-yard line, needed a touchdown to win yet had seventy-five yards to go. The coach sent in a play. It was a sideline pass to Tyler, but he needed to get out of bounds and stop the clock. Tyler ran along the sideline, looking over his right shoulder for the spiral. Soaring high for the ball keeping his feet in bounds, he caught the ball.

"Yow!" Michael yelled. "A fifty-yard pass play! Just what the doctor ordered!" As Tyler got up slowly, because of the icy field, he could hardly feel any sensation in his hands. He noticed they were turning blue. He always rejected the idea of gloves since he believed they interfered with the "feel" of the ball.

Then he saw something that caused him to stop dead in his tracks. Among the cheering throng on the sideline, he noticed someone wrapped up in a fur collared hooded overcoat. He could see a long black beard that blended into auburn fur around the hood. "That's my dad!" he said to himself. As he jogged back to the huddle, he kept looking over his shoulder toward the sideline. He felt like running up to his father, hugging him then hanging on to him for dear life and never letting him go.

In the huddle, the quarterback shouted, "This is it! No more time-outs! We have to score, damn it! 58 boot-leg pass. Walden! The pass is to you! Be sure you brush-block the end first!"

Tyler came off the ball quickly and hit the charging defensive end to slow his speed. Then he threw a beautiful head fake on the safety, did a down and out, and found himself standing all alone in the right corner of the end zone totally open. He raised up his arms, jumping up and down and screaming, "Throw me the ball! Throw me the ball!"

Suddenly, a perfect spiral was delivered by the quarterback. Tyler could hear the footsteps of an approaching defensive back. Then he heard someone yell, "Catch that son of a bitch! Catch it!" He turned his head in the direction of the voice. Just then the ball hit him on the numbers on his jersey and bounced out of bounds.

A penetrating silence permeated the crowd. The game was lost and as far as they were concerned Tyler Walden blew it. The silence of the crowd didn't last long, though. Soon there was a chorus of boos. As the team ran into the lockers, the boos grew louder. He heard someone in crowd say, "The hooker's kid…he's the one that lost it!" Young Tyler Walden was devastated.

CHAPTER TWELVE

September–1995–Bridgetown

Even though Tyler was not her biological child, Molly Winslow showered him with affection. When Tyler entered his adolescent years, she became perplexed and blamed herself for what she considered his social awkwardness. She regularly implored him to get more involved with his peers by participating in extracurricular activities at school. But when she brought the subject up, Tyler would feel letdown and would retreat to his bedroom. He practically lived there, studying hard and reading just about anything he could get his hands on.

But now Wayne and Molly had a much bigger issue to address and were very alarmed. It was the Monday evening following the game, when the Bridgetown Titans football team lost the county championship to the Belmont Blue Devils.

"Tyler has been away from home for two nights," Molly said. "I've called all his friends and they have no idea where he is. In the past, when he has been late, he would always call us. Something must have happened to him! I'm getting really scared!"

"The police have been looking for him." Wayne said. "I'm struggling with myself. I don't believe Tyler would disappear just because he dropped a pass in the end zone near the end of the game."

"Wayne, it's not just that he dropped a pass! That boy believes he lost the game! He also got booed at the end of the game. My heart was broken when I heard those boos. What a tough pill to swallow for a thirteen-year-old!"

Wayne remembered the adage that was in last week's homily at his church. "Those who applaud you on Palm Sunday will crucify you on Good Friday," he said. "You know, people can be extremely cruel, Molly."

"He's just a young boy." Molly stood up from her chair, walked to the fireplace mantel, and buried her face in her arm and sobbed.

"The kid can't just run away from life's disappointments!" Wayne said. "I know I can help him with this. Even the men in our group come to me with their problems. Why can't he?"

Molly was still sobbing. "Poor kid. He must be in great pain."

"I'd like to think he would come home and want to be consoled by us," Wayne said. "Maybe I'm naïve but I thought we were the closest people to him."

"In addition to Jeff, we probably are," Molly said. "Don't forget, he is very angry at his parents for abandoning him. And he really hates Billy with a deep passion!"

"Oh, my God! That's it!"

"What's the matter?" Wayne asked.

He's going after Billy!" Molly cried. "I just know it! That's why he's not home. He despises him and blames him for everything! We must find him now! Billy will hurt him!"

"Okay. I'm calling Michael right now!" he said. "I just wonder how many more setbacks this kid can handle." Wayne shook his head in dismay.

CHAPTER THIRTEEN

September 1995 - Bridgetown

When Wayne contacted Michael, he eagerly volunteered to call Francine. Whether it was conscious or subliminal, the possibility of another few hours of ecstasy with her was irresistible. He realized Tyler would never stay with his mother after all that she had done to embarrass him.

When he called Francine, however, there was no answer. Now, he thought, I have the perfect excuse to go over to see her again.

But he had to proceed cautiously. Falling asleep in his office was an alibi that worked once but wouldn't fly a second time. Also, he realized Megan was getting suspicious because of how distant he had become around the house. He knew she had cause for alarm, but the apparent depth of his love for Francine was all-consuming.

And then there were issues fomenting in his office. Fantasizing about Francine while addressing the needs of his clients was starting to alienate them.

"You just aren't with it, Michael," William Forsythe said, one of his best clients. "What the hell's going on in your head? I can't afford your indifference when managing my money."

Three days later, Michael's secretary, Jenny, walked into Michael's office with a liquidation notice. "Got some bad news, Michael. Bill Forsythe transferred two million dollars to Grant Adams."

That got Michael's attention. "Now why the hell would he do that without checking with me first?"

"Maybe he doesn't think you care anymore," Jenny said with a rare display of boldness. "He sent a note. Want to read it?" "Yes, dammit!" Michael read the note aloud.

Dear Michael,

We've had a long productive relationship and I apologize for moving my money to Grant's investment firm. But, my good friend, I'm afraid you've been sleeping at the switch.

My retirement account still has too much volatility for a retired old bird like me. A month ago, you said you would transfer my assets to a conservative portfolio, yet when I checked, I still had mostly aggressive stocks. Maybe this will serve as awake up call for you.

You are a good financial advisor, Michael, but lately your head has not been in the game. I'm sorry but, at my age, I can't afford the losses.
Sincerely,
Bill Forsythe

"Jen, do you think what he is saying is true?"

Jen leaned over his desk. "I'm sorry Michael. Yes, I do," she said wistfully.

"She handed Michael another letter. This one was from her announcing her resignation.

"Jen! Not you too! How come? What's the problem?"

"I just couldn't turn down the offer from Grant Adams. Michael, it's a fifty percent increase in pay and being a single parent, I can use the money."

"Jen, please tell me something…why didn't you come to me before you spoke with Grant? After all our years together, I thought we had more rapport between us."

"I appreciate that, Michael, but it really wouldn't have made a difference. I'm not sure I know you anymore. I'm sorry but it's no longer fun or challenging to work for you."

On the way home that night, Michael engaged in some serious soul searching. His first thought was Megan. Obviously, his relationship with Francine was totally unfair to Megan and she did not deserve his infidelity, certainly not after all the years they have been together.

And my kids…I can't face them anymore. The idea of not hearing the word "Daddy" everyday would be a crushing blow. Then there is the inescapable fact that I really loved Francine. I didn't want to be in love with her. But the dye has been cast. I crossed the Rubicon and my feelings were firmly implanted deep inside of me.

Suddenly, he had a mental hiccup. Really? he said to himself. Other than being a good lay, I hardly know the woman. Sure, I know her reputation, but that was a different Francine, the one who was emotionally unstable, the derelict mother and wife. She is an entirely changed woman now.

However, there would be consequences…many of which were impossible to identify right now but…wait a minute. Now that Jenny is leaving the practice, I do need clerical help. I'll offer the job to Francine. If she accepts, I wouldn't have to leave Megan. Francine and

I would be together eight to ten hours a day. That's more time than I spend with Megan in a week!

In the meantime, things were also deteriorating at home and Megan was beginning to vocalize her concerns. "Michael," she said with a growing irritation, "you're a million miles away. Wherever you are, please come back! The kids and I are starting to feel very insignificant."

But Michael tried hard to repel his feelings. "I'm sorry, Honey. I've got a lot of things on my mind from work. I just lost one of my best clients and Jenny is quitting."

"I'm not surprised. What's going on with you, Michael? We have always trusted one another with the truth. Now, tell me, what is it?"

Michael came close to telling her about his experience with Francine. I'll get it off my back and be done with it! At the last second, he backed off. She'd throw me out! Thoughts of his children filled his mind. Suddenly, he felt shameful and very displeased with himself. He never viewed himself as a liar and a cheater, yet he knew that's exactly what he had become.

I just must live with it, he conceded to himself. I'm certainly not ready to give up my relationship with Francine…not under any circumstances!

When Michael went over to Francine's, ostensibly to check on Tyler's whereabouts, he eagerly anticipated another carnal adventure with her. The wooden stairs to the apartment were unsteady. I'll have to have these fixed for her. Just then a screeching Amtrak passenger train raced by on the adjacent tracks startling him.

It was dark and scary. Street lights were a luxury in this part of town. Only one small light could be seen through the kitchen window.

He rang the doorbell then knocked. Maybe I'll just turn the door knob and see what happens. To his surprise, the door wasn't locked. Michael walked into the kitchen area slowly. He walked through the almost pitch-black hallway approaching her bedroom. Soft love making music, was almost inaudible. He pushed open the door cautiously. There she was… on the right-hand side of the bed, facing the right wall, exactly where she was the morning they made passionate love. She's in bed waiting for me, he assumed. Perfect! He walked very quietly around to the left side of the bed, removed his shirt and trousers, drew back the covers, and crawled in next to her. Starting with her back, he began kissing and caressing her naked body. When he reached over her shoulder and attempted to turn her upper body toward him, he realized something was terribly wrong.

"Francine!" Maybe she had crashed on cocaine but as he reached for her he felt the blood that had pooled on her chest and panicked, jumping out of the bed and falling on the floor. A frozen chill heaved threw his veins and up the back of his neck. He grabbed one of the bedposts, stood up and looked at Francine bleeding profusely in bed.

"No! No!" he cried out. A large knife wound in her chest was visible when he checked her pulse. She was dead. He was sure of that. He stood above the bed staring down on her body, losing track of reality, so mortified he almost lost consciousness.

Then he heard someone was shuffling in the hallway, someone trying hard not to be heard. Michael moved guardedly. The hallway was vacant, but the front door was wide open, as if someone was too much in a rush to close it.

He decided to call 911. As soon as he picked up the phone, he felt extreme pain radiating from his back, traversing his neck, and then penetrating his chest. No longer did he have control of his senses or his physical stability. He collapsed, slamming his head into a wooden table top as he fell. Writhing in the worst kind of agony he had ever experienced, he rolled over on the floor screaming in a futile attempt to dispel the pain that would not go away until he finally passed out.

Chapter Fourteen

September – 1995 – Francine's Bridgetown Apartment

Michael's skull was pounding as if someone had unloaded a pallet of concrete masonry bricks on his head. He was nauseous and dizzy and wondered what the hell had happened to him. Lying flat on the living room sofa, the ice pack on his head did not help much. Although his vision was somewhat foggy, he could see white coats everywhere. As he became more aware, he assumed the forensic team had already started their investigation into Francine's murder. Michael looked at his watch. It was 3:00 a.m. He tried getting up, but a big hand gently pushed him back on the couch.

"Whoa there, brother! You are in no condition to move!" a gruff but familiar voice declared. Chief Lefty Margolis was placing a fresh ice pack behind his head.

"Just keep your ass still and your mouth shut until the pain wears off and you feel like telling me what the fuck you were doing here without your clothes on!"

Michael was in no mood to be quiet. Slowly he was recalling Francine's dead body. It must have been a bad nightmare. When he saw them take Francine out in a yellow body bag on a gurney, he knew he wasn't dreaming. Suddenly, he broke down and started to weep.

"Lover's tears?" Lefty asked. "You of all people!"

"Bullshit! Just tell me what the hell happened to me?" he sniveled, trying hard not to make it too obvious.

The chief had his chin pointed upwards with a cigar in his mouth, apparently to look more authoritative, or just to intimidate Michael.

"Hmm," he said. "Seems like one of my boys, Thomas Trescott, tasered your ass. He got here first and thought you were the killer. Just doin' his job, that's all."

"C'mon man! You've got to be kidding! Don't 'your boys' ask any questions first?"

"Listen, goddamn it! There's a killer stalking people in this area! No! They don't ask questions first! It's too damn risky. And why the hell were you here in the first place? Let's start with that question!"

"I was looking for Tyler Waldon. He never came home after the game. His parents asked me to intervene." Michael adjusted the ice pack on his head wincing as he moved it. "Just thought maybe he'd be at his mother's place."

"Why the 'birthday suit'?"

"Listen, Lefty, I can explain!"

"You listen to me! You know goddamn well that kid would never go to his mother! Any other reason you might be here?" The chief's smirk said it all.

"Look, Michael, you're in the house naked, a woman is dead in the bed, what the fuck would you think if you were in my shoes?"

"I know it looks incriminating. But it is ridiculous to assume I had anything to do with her murder. It just made sense that a boy in need of affection and understanding just might want his mother."

"It's not so ridiculous to assume you killed her, is it? In fact, it is much more ridiculous to assume you didn't! If I might be so crass as to ask, why are your clothes off? You still have not told me. Your answer better be good or I'm booking you for first degree murder."

Michael knew he couldn't talk his way around this one, so he told Lefty the truth. Megan would probably find out because Lefty had such a big mouth.

"First, I have absolutely no motive to kill her. We were having an affair. I had fallen in love with her and attempted to surprise her when I found her in bed." Michael's voice quivered. "I had no idea she was dead. But my first intention was to come here and see if Tyler was here."

"Looks like one of my boys got here first!" The chief smiled smugly.

"Guess so! The son-of-a-bitch!"

"Calm down. Calm down. It was a routine accident."

"Routine? You have the nerve to tell me tasering the wrong person is 'routine'?" Michael wondered how many other innocent people had been tasered by one of 'his boys'.

"Let's talk about your boy…that Jeff Walden character," the chief said."

"Okay. Michael nodded compliantly. "Let's do that."

"Right now, he's the guy. We think he did it."

"No way! Kill Francine? His son's mother? His own wife?" Michael exclaimed. "No way!"

"Before you fly off the handle, let me just tell you this. First off, he was here. His fingerprints are all over…in the hallway, in the kitchen, and in the bedroom…"

"You realize, of course, Lefty, he used to live here, right?" Michael was baffled that the chief would arrive at that conclusion on his own.

"Of course, I do!" The chief did not like to be second-guessed "You think I'm stupid? I told you…thirty-five years I've been doing this! We already factored that into our thinking. But, for your information, there are several fresh prints in the kitchen and bedroom areas."

"What the hell is a 'fresh print'?

Lefty completely ignored the question.

"We need to check the murder weapon too. We know it was a razor-sharp knife. When we find it, and we will find it, it will be checked for fingerprints and blood type. My boys have searched all over this place and are now out on the railroad tracks checking the tallgrass on the shoulders."

Now that's a real stretch, Michael thought. Finding anything out there was like trying to find a contact lens in a pile of sand.

"Let me know if you find it, okay?" he said thinking they never will. And even if they do, it can't possibly have Jeff's prints on it.

The chief hesitated a few seconds, looking straight at Michael. "I'm not excited giving out information that could be used as evidence. Let's see what the search turns up and we'll go from there. Killers don't hide murder weapons in obvious places, but like I said, I will find it!"

Michael nodded. "By the way, did you find that maniac who raped that girl and beat up that guy up in the Romano Sandpits?"

"Right now, Jeff is our best suspect."

"C'mon Lefty! You have no evidence to support that! Did 'your boys' thoroughly search the sandpits like you said they would?"

"Michael! Goddamn it, I always do what I say I'm going to do! They searched it high and low every which way." He swiveled his cigar nervously side to side in his mouth. "There are many secluded areas up there to hide and they tell me they searched them all."

More Bullshit! At this point, after being needlessly tasered by a deputy, Michael's impressions of the police department were gravely tarnished. I don't believe the sandpits were even searched, let alone searched effectively. And I have no confidence in the chief's leadership abilities. It sounded like the chief took 'his boys' word for everything without challenging them or expecting better results from them. At least, for now, the chief decided not to press charges against me, thank the Lord!

Following a cursory physical examination by one the doctors present, Michael departed. His head hurt but his pride hurt more. As he drove home, he couldn't prevent his hand from shaking. Grief was taking hold. Michael's eyes filled with tears again partly because of the trauma he experienced, but mostly because the full impact of Francine's death was beginning to sink in. It made him realize just how much he cared for her.

Strangely, Michael also had a feeling of inexplicable relief. Misery and heartache replaced the shame that clutched his body during the last several days. Now he had to prepare himself to deal with Megan's reaction when she found out. And, he knew she would find out. Most of Bridgetown's gossip mongers would have the information in the coffee and barber shops by the end of the week. It was just the way a small town like Bridgetown operated.

But, right now, Michael had more important matters to address.

When he arrived home, he found Megan sitting up in bed with her arms folded with an alarming almost desperate look on her face.

"Where the hell were you all night?" Megan asked, with more than a little unease. "What in God's name happened to your head? You have a gigantic red mark on the left side of your head! Did you get into a fight?"

"I'm so sorry, honey." After he explained how he was inadvertently tasered by a reckless deputy and was unconscious for several hours, Janet seemed to accept his story. "Now Jeff will be blamed for Francine's murder and sent to prison for life…or worse. I must get involved now! I just can't allow this to happen! Jeff is not a murderer!"

"Did you find young Tyler?" she asked. "That was the purpose of your going there, right?"

Michael stammered. "Ah, yes, of course it was. But the answer is no"

"So, where do you think young Tyler is?" she asked.

"My gut tells me he's with Jeff."

As he placed his head on the pillow, a parade of emotions marched inside his brain: sorrow for Francine, fear, that some killer was loose, and that the local police were way too inept to catch him. Remorse, that young Tyler Walden lost his mother and probably doesn't even know it. Anger, that Jeff is still incognito. That emotion opened a Pandora's box of other questions. Is Tyler with him? If so, where the hell are they? Will Tyler be back in school on Monday? Is the fat guy still with Jeff? What about Billy? Did he have anything to do with Francine's murder? Oh, yes. There was also that guy Igor who would probably arrive soon.

CHAPTER FIFTEEN

September - 1995 - Bridgetown

Michael responded to Coach Winslow's early morning phone call by meeting him at the coach's office at 7 a.m., two days after he discovered Francine's dead body.

Still trembling, Michael couldn't remove the image of Francine's blood laden body on her bed. In his subconscious mind, if he heard it once, he heard it thousand times. "One of my boys tasered you." He still felt muscle spasms and was afraid there might be some neurological damage.

He learned from the morning newspaper that Thomas Trescott, one of Lefty's deputies was credited with the taser assault.

But, what really bothered Michael was that Margolis didn't seem to give a damn, like it was some sort of achievement to taser the wrong person.

Michael pretty much convinced himself that if anyone was going to find Jeff and Tyler, it would be him. He needed to step-up and get more involved.

When he walked through the athletic area, he was impressed with all the young men working out in the weight room so early on a Sunday morning.

The gym was full of basketball players. Folded bleachers provided more space so that four games could be played on the short courts simultaneously. This is an example of Coach Winslow's leadership, he surmised.

The coach wasn't in his office so when Michael arrived he examined the trophies on the shelves especially those received for the county football championship over the last few years. This year's trophy will be conspicuous by its absence. Too bad, he thought with regret.

Then his eyes found a commemorative plaque on the far wall. He could not avoid it since it was the only one on the wall and was inscribed with big gold letters that said:

> Perfection is not attainable,
> but if we chase perfection
> we can catch excellence.
> -Vince Lombardi

Michael read the words a few times. Just then, Coach Winslow walked in and sat behind his desk.

"I love that quote from Lombardi. That plaque was given to me by the Bridgetown Chamber of Commerce after we won our first county championship five years ago."

Wayne spoke softly and smiled cordially. But Michael could see uneasiness and distress on his face.

"Sorry for being late, Mike. How are you, my friend? Missed you at the men's group meeting last week."

"Had a rough few nights, Coach. Actually, I thought I was going to be spend the first night with Lefty locked up for murder."

"I know. That's why I called you. We had a very tearful night. My wife and I didn't sleep two winks."

"How did you find out, Wayne?"

"I called the chief to see if he had any information on Tyler. He explained what happened. I called you after that. I know you would never raise a finger to hurt that woman. What a horrifying way to die."

"I appreciate that. So, the chief told you the whole story?"

"Well, he told me about the gruesome way she died." Wayne put his head down staring at papers on his desk then looked up directly at Michael. "You must be devastated, Michael."

"I'm worse that devastated. I had fallen in love with Francine."

Wayne leaned back in his chair and sighed. "In love? Oh, really. May I ask you how you arrived at that conclusion?"

"How does anyone arrive at that type of conclusion?" Michael asked testily.

"Is it a feeling?"

"Of course. What else could it be?" Michael was beginning to get rattled.

"Well, I don't know, but as long as you are asking me, I think love is more than that."

"I'm sick to my stomach and scared to death that Megan will find out. I feel so guilty because I betrayed the people I love. I'll never get over it. One moment I'm lost in thoughts of how exciting our love making was. In the next moment, I feel shamed beyond belief to the point where I almost hate her."

"Let me ask you…other than sleeping with her, how well do you know her?"

"About as well as you do," Michael said.

"But I'm not in love with her."

"Why would you be?"

"That's exactly my point. I didn't sleep with her! Are you confusing sexual passion with love? It's easy to do. You need to lock that reality into your brain or you are going to suffer great emotional stress. You also need to come clean with Megan. You chance of rectifying the situation is much greater if you tell her instead of her finding from the notorious Bridgetown grapevine."

"Please excuse me for a minute," Michael said. "I need to use the men's room."

"Over there to the left." Wayne directed.

After Michael locked himself into one of the men's room stalls, he sat down and cried his eyes out. *I need to snap out this funk I am in. Wayne is right. There is no way I could be truly in love with that woman. No way!*

When Michael returned, Wayne moved from behind his desk to a chair adjacent to where Michael was sitting. He leaned forward to make closer eye contact.

"I've been sitting here thinking about what your dilemma. Since you came to me Michael, I want to be completely honest with you. When I think of your beautiful and devoted wife, and your two exquisite children, I must tell you, Michael, you really have you head right up your ass! What really pisses me off is Molly and I have been trying for years to have children. Sorry to be so blunt, but you should be grateful. Michael, I always viewed you as a pillar of the community, a leader and role model. How could you have fallen prey to the town slut? For Christ sake! Remember? You were the one who recommended Tyler to us because of the abuse he was experiencing with Francine! Do you remember all the evidence my lawyer uncovered during the custody hearings?"

"Of course, I do. I didn't come here for a tongue lashing, Wayne."

"Well, you shouldn't have come here at all then! What happened with Tyler this weekend, his mother's murder, and now this? Sorry if I find it all very difficult to wrap my arms around."

"She's gone."

"Get over it!"

"Who do you think committed the murder?" Michael asked wishing the subject would change.

"Billy! Who else could possibly have a reason to kill her?"

"So, Wayne, what do you think was his motive?" Michael asked.

"Are you kidding, Michael? I'm totally shocked that you feel a need to ask me that question! You know as well as I do that Billy is the son-of-bitch who beat her into submitting to prostitution. He physically abused her every day and then turned his anger on Tyler, an innocent kid trying to deal with all the turmoil in his life. And now, I understand, Francine was trying to clean up her act to regain custody of Tyler! It would have been over my goddamn dead body!" Wayne's voice became several octaves higher.

To Michael, Wayne's vehemence seemed way out of character. Known for his serenity and self-control, his exasperation seemed to spill into a pool of hatefulness and rage. What a change of tone, he thought.

Michael pressed on. "Did you know Francine had a restraining order in place?"

"Of course, I knew! Do you really think that would stop a lunatic like Billy? It certainly didn't stop him from killing her, did it?"

"I'm not sure Billy killed her," Michael argued. "The crime just happened last night. Don't you think we should let the authorities complete their due diligence before we jump to any conclusions?"

"Yeah, I guess you're right," Wayne conceded. "You let them perform their 'due diligence' as you say. But if I see that bastard, I'll kill him myself!"

"I'll forget you ever said that Wayne."

"I'm sorry, for going off like that but Molly and I are so upset. We never in a million years believed Tyler would run away. We've done so much for that kid!"

Michael returned home with a severe migraine headache. Instead of alleviating his guilt, Wayne worsened it. He had to get out of Bridgetown for a while. The debilitating effect of Francine's murder and his inability to grieve openly was making him sick.

Despite strong objections from Megan, Michael was determined to go to Schroon Lake. I need to get away from it all and have some private time and get my head screwed right. Maybe Jeff is back in his cabin at the lake. I think I'll take a drive up there and see."

But Megan had to get some things off of her chest. "Michael," she said emphatically, "I am having serious difficulties trying to figure out why you are so duty-bound to find Jeff and Tyler in the first place. After all, they are not part of our family. In fact, the more I think about it, the more resentful I am becoming. Your obsession to find them is tearing our family apart. Listen, Michael, you have been mentally detached and now you will be physically detached as well. I just can't stand this anymore! We need to have a serious 'Come to Jesus Meeting.' You and me! I think you blew a fuse and I don't know why. You are so different! I don't feel you care anymore… about the kids, about me, your career and our life together. All you can focus on is finding two people who really don't matter that much in our lives. The boys feel alienated by their father and I have no idea what to tell them. Can you give me a clue? We really deserve an explanation, Michael!"

As Megan spoke, Michael dropped his head in a woeful gaze. He knew she had a right to be upset. But that didn't change his mind.

"I'll be back in a few days and we will sit down and discuss it, okay?" he said, attempting to side step the issue, at least, for the time being.

But Megan wouldn't yield. "I'd like to talk about it right now!" she said heatedly. "You keep putting these issues on the back burner and I'm tired of trying to guess what the hell is going on with you!"

"I promise I will bring this up the moment I get home."

Megan leered at him angrily. She had run out of patience and was in no mood for any more excuses.

"Actually, you know what?" she said. "Don't bother coming home at all! I'm done dealing with this!" She left the room slamming the door behind her.

While Michael was distressed, he figured she would get over it in a few days. She always did when she was angry. Ironically, however, this time, he didn't care if she got over it or not. He knew he had some serious family damage control to attend to, but with all the anguish in his heart, he was much too emotionally paralyzed to deal with it now.

Maybe by being alone in the Schroon Lake house for a while, I will have chance for some solitary meditation, so I can get my messed-up head square, then prepare myself to deal with things on the home front.

Michael took his time driving to Schroon Lake. He drove slowly in the right-hand lane, allowing other vehicles to whiz by him at twice the speed.

At first, his mind was empty, devoid of any contemplations whatsoever. Soon, the rhythm of the road stirred his thoughts. Evaluating his behavior over the last several weeks led to nothing but bewilderment. In one sense, I feel extreme guilt. In another, I feel strangely liberated, as if I broke the chains of a lackluster life and branched out into new territory. One thing was for sure. Wayne was right. I used to pride myself on my righteousness. But now all that is gone. I feel a loss of innocence, a resounding guilt, and a seriously impaired self-confidence. Maybe that's why I need to go to Schroon Lake and find those guys. The emotional upheaval I experienced over Francine, the affair and then her death, has had an irrepressible affect me. I need to return to the "me" I really am.

Chapter Sixteen

September- 1995–Schroon Lake

Once Michael arrived in Schroon Lake, he decided to check in at Ray's Fish Shack for any scuttlebutt on Jeff and also to catch an early dinner.

Ray was preparing food for the small number of patrons that usually showed up for dinner.

"Michael! Nice to see you! What brings you up here this time of the year?"

"A man has to eat," Michael smiled.

"Amen to that!" Ray laughed. "A man has to drink too. What will you have, Mike?"

"Bud Light."

"Perfect!"

"Listen, Mike, I got some huge Yellow Perch that were just brought in. I'm fryin' up some right now in cornmeal, peanut oil, with a touch of garlic. Should be ready in about ten minutes or so."

"Sounds great to me, Ray! Throw in some onions too, would you please?"

"Sure thing, Mike. You got it! How 'bout some potatoes and carrots?"

"I'll take it!" The aroma from the frying fish was too appetizing to resist.

Michael already felt good about his decision to 'get away from it all'. He had forgotten how much he enjoyed hanging out in the Schroon Lake area. The scenery, the spontaneity, the untroubled lifestyle in the mountains has never been more appealing.

Had Francine not been murdered, I would have taken her up here, he thought. We could have stayed at my place. He started to choke up as he recalled the image of Francine standing over him that night in her apartment. She was a beautiful woman for sure, he reveled, then he quickly altered his feelings before he broke down in tears front of Ray.

"Hey Ray…tell me something. That guy Snork…does he still hang here?"

"Haven't seen the tons of fun lately, Mike. Can't really say I miss the fatso either. He is what I call a shit disturber. It's kind of like everything is going well and he'll make some smart-ass remark to someone and next thing I know, I've got World War III on my hands."

"How 'bout Jeff? Has he been here?"

"You mean my buddy, Festus?"

"Yeah, Festus," Michael repeated.

"I think that guy has disappeared off the face of the earth. Before he was injured on Rt. 9, I'd see him almost every day. On weekends, he'd bring in a shit load of Salmon and Trout and my customers loved it. I wish he'd come back. Sometimes, his brother, Billy, shows up here and let me tell you, he ain't nothin' like Festus. He looks like a real shit-heal, someone who's always pissed off at the world. He sits over there in the corner with an attitude and usually keeps his trap shut. I never knew who the hell he was until he tried to screw me out of dinner one night and I had him arrested."

"What the hell is Billy doing up here in Schroon Lake?" Michael asked totally bewildered. He hadn't seen nor heard from Billy in several months. "Ray, do you know where the hell he is?"

"Townsfolk say he is staying at Festus' place on the lake. Yeah, I guess he's been up here ever since Festus' accident. Billy, let me tell you, the guy's a real opportunist. At first, I thought he was here to visit Festus in the hospital, but when Festus vanished like a small fart in a big wind storm Billy moved in like he owned the place! It's gonna be another Thrilla in Manila when Jeff gets healthy and finds out."

Michael was speechless. This doesn't pass the smell test! The bloody hate between the brothers didn't allow for sleep-overs. Furthermore, Michael was unaware Billy knew about Jeff's hideaway. That bastard! I'll bet he had something to do with Jeff's disappearance. Maybe he really did kill Francine too!

A sudden surge of adrenalin rushed through Michael's veins. "Do you think Billy knows where his brother is?" he asked Ray.

"Well, I can tell you this…if he was my brother I certainly would know," Ray replied. "I'd be watching my back every minute!"

Michael ordered another Bud Light and downed it hurriedly. He practically inhaled the fried Perch. "Really good, Ray! I have to go!"

"What's the rush, Mike? I got some great tiramisu! Made it myself!"

"Can't wait! Have to go to the cabin and see if I can find Billy," he said impatiently. There's much more than meets the eye here. And I'm going to find out what it is!"

Ray stood in awe of Michael's frenzied state. "Take it easy, Mike, the cabin will be there tomorrow. Have another drink and relax a little."

"Can't!" Michael exclaimed. "Have to go!" With that, Michael paid Ray for dinner and exited the restaurant as if he had to rescue someone from a raging inferno.

The expanse of water between Jeff's cabin and the Garden of Eden Shoreline was only about a hundred yards. Although the weather was ominous, small waves dispersed rapidly as they reached the shore and the wind died down to slight breeze.

In front of the Garden of Eden Shoreline, a half dozen true to life Mallard decoys floated serenely. With a myriad of different postures and their ultra-realistic paint schemes, it was difficult to believe they were fake.

Billy Walden waited patiently inside the well-camouflaged duck blind back about twenty yards from the shoreline. His light complexion, yellowish brown hair, and flaxen facial hair was covered by a four-piece Ghillie suit that had a woodland camouflage appearance. The suit included a jacket, pants, gun wrap, and facemask. His large physique looked even larger not only because of his Ghillie suit but because his steel plated bullet proof vest he purchased on eBay, provided extra bulk.

But Billy wasn't interested in mere waterfowl. He would love to put a bullet between the eyes of that thousand-pound bull moose he saw the other day swimming toward Jeff's cabin, the one Jeff calls "Eli". He said to himself I could sell that rack for big money and the venison… it would keep me fat through the winter, not to mention the hide from that beast could warm my ass when it gets twenty below up here. My Ak-47 rifle might tear the shit out of him but what the fuck…

who the hell cares! It really packs a wallop, especially if I use my new hollow point shells. I'll bet I could blow the horns right off that sucker!

Billy looked down at the ground. There was another rifle resting on a pile of leaves. I'm done fuckin' around. This .30-30 Winchester's gonna see some action today! Maybe I can pick off some assholes hangin' around the beach! Maybe I can murder them sitting in their backyards. They ain't never going to find me here in this stupid blind my dumb ass brother built.

I ain't got no good fuckin reason to live anymore anyway… except for Francine. She made some good money for me. Just might try to talk her into it again. Maybe she would marry me, that is, if I ever get back to Bridgetown. But now I can't see her because of that goddamn restraining order and I know Michael Alexander was behind that. I'm really getting sick and tired of people – all people! Especially, my numskull brother who hasn't got a clue!

Billy checked his twelve-inch Bowie combat knife tucked away in his hip sheath and he began to scan the area with a set of powerful binoculars.

He looked at Jeff's cabin. Shit! I left the front door open! Wait a minute! A new BMW pulled up and parked behind the cabin. A man got out and walked toward the open door. Billy gritted his teeth in anger. I hate that bastard! He lifted the Winchester and pointed it toward door. Michael was in his sights. All he had to do is pull the trigger and Michael was a dead man. Instead, he hesitated just long enough for Michael to walk through the door. I'll get that SOB when he leaves!

Michael entered the cabin hoping to find Billy and secure information about Jeff's whereabouts. Instead, he discovered a messy and musty lived-in residence that smelled of human body odor. Stale food was strewn all over the floor and the first thought that crossed Michael's mind was how can one person make such a mess? Then it occurred to him that maybe there was more than one person living in the cabin. Anything is possible with Billy, he thought.

Michael walked outside and looked around the beach for any sign of Billy. The boat is gone so Billy must be out on the water fishing. I'll hang here for a while.

Billy still had his Winchester pointed in the direction of the cabin. He made a minor target adjustment as Michael walked to an outside lawn chair. His finger bent to squeeze the trigger. "Now I got this son-of-bitch!" he said.

Abruptly, without warning, a figure hurdled over the rear barricade of the blind and landed on top of Billy who crashed to the ground hard. Dazed and amazed he cried, "You son of…" Before he could get the words out, he was clocked with a measured blow from a leather covered blackjack. Billy was unconscious. He was carried to the boat that was parked behind the duck blind, his hands tied with two nylon zip ties. The boat sped off making a large wake that totally discombobulated the Mallard decoys.

CHAPTER SEVENTEEN

September-1995-Schroon Lake and Mt. Defiance

An offshore gust of wind agitated the small twigs and leaves in front of Jeff's cabin into a blustery swirl. Dark clouds blocked what little sunshine remained. The gloomy weather matched the melancholy Michael felt as an incredible surge of loneliness flooded his consciousness. The wooden bench he had been sitting on started to feel like a slab of concrete. After two hours of waiting, without any sign of Billy, he was ready to call it day and go to his place.

A heavy rain pounded his windshield as Michael entered his car. Then, he sat motionless resting his arms on the steering wheel glaring aimlessly at the lake.

I can't go on without her, he said to himself. I don't know how to reprogram myself and get my life back.

Megan's words resonated in his mind:

"You are so different! I don't feel you care anymore… about the kids, about me, your career, our life together."

His head slumped forward as he cupped his eyes in the palm of his hands and started to sob. He sobbed for the beautiful young woman with whom he had fallen in love. And, the woman needlessly killed in the prime of her life. He sobbed for his emotional turmoil and the pain it was causing his family, especially Megan.

Oh God! I must snap out of this! I've got way too much at stake to be so consumed by something I cannot change.

It was unlike Michael to be so down on himself. His grief was overwhelming enough but combined with his self-incrimination, he felt as if his head was in a vice and someone was cranking the handle tighter and tighter. He had become so totally absorbed in his personal agony over his loss of Francine, he felt it eradicated all that was good and worthwhile in his life.

A loud crack of thunder, then a piercing streak of lightning quickly jolted him from his despondency. He regained enough composure to start his car and drive to his summer vacation home, just a few miles up the road from Jeff's cabin. He relished thoughts of two or three perfect Manhattans. Anything to ease the pain, he thought. Maybe I can knock myself out with some whiskey and get through the night.

As soon as he arrived at his vacation home, Michael literally saturated himself with Manhattans and ascended to an advanced state of intoxication in record time. He collapsed on the sofa as he was staggering toward his bedroom. The pain gone, it was replaced by a strange numbness and a blurry picture of a large room packed with memories.

He remembered last Christmas when his two boys were sitting on the floor opening Christmas gifts. "Hey Dad, Jason shouted. Look what Santa brought me... the new ski's I wanted!" Megan was in the kitchen preparing Christmas dinner and occasionally walked over and kissed and caressed him. He felt a sense of fulfillment and gratification. The people he loved were with him.

At sunrise Michael was awakened by a pillow thoroughly soaked with perspiration and the bothersome sound of squawking seagulls collecting on the rear dock. He winced with pain as he planted one hand on each side of his face. I have the worst damn migraine. The thumping pain in his head was making him so nauseous, he spent the next hour in the bathroom retching. When he finally got cleaned up and dressed, he decided to head over to Ray's Fish Shack for breakfast and perhaps catch up on any news on Jeff or Billy.

When he arrived, a 1943 WW II Jeep was parked sideways near the front door. With its Army green, white markings, and stars and stripes flying majestically from a long pole attached to the rear deck, one might conclude General Patton was having breakfast with the boys.

Michael pulled up in his BMW and parked next to the Jeep and for a moment thought how neat it would be to own one just like it. I would quit my job, set up residence on the beach, and fish and drink all day long just like Jeff. No more problems. No more drama. It didn't take long for him to snap out his short-lived fantasy, but it felt good while it lasted.

The Snork emerged from Ray's just as Michael was entering. "Like your Jeep!" Michael quipped.

"Cool, huh? Mary Jane is some ride alright! A Japanese hand grenade exploded right near the front grill. Never had her repaired. She got me through the last days of the fighting on Iwo and then I slipped her on a troop ship to the states. If you ride in her, she'll parch your gonads for sure, but you'll get used to the old girl! And unlike my old buckboard, you don't have to smell a horse shit either!"

"That's a definite advantage!" Michael enjoyed a good laugh. It felt good. "Mind telling me where you're headed?" he asked.

"Gotta go check up on my pal Festus! He's probably still racked up in his crib!"

"May I ride along?" Michael asked nonchalantly. "It's been a while since I've seen my good buddy, Jeff."

"Okay with me!" The Snork replied. Michael jumped into the Jeep and The Snork drove off as if he was escaping from a group of Zeros on Iwo.

"No seatbelts, huh?"

"Shit no! Seatbelts are for pussies!"

"Hey Snork… just for shits and giggles…mind telling me where the hell you are from?"

"I'm an old 'jack' from the way up north. I was also a 'road monkey' and can still hear the roars and the purrs from those old 'cat crawlers'. I drove a Linn tractor. Did you ever hear of one?"

"Can't say that I have."

"With their new gas engines, man were they powerful! Beat the shit out of the horses, I'll tell you that! And boy, no one messed with them 'jacks'. They had hearts of gold but don't cross them. Piss off one, you piss 'em all off and that ain't good!"

"What brought you to this area?" Michael asked.

Snork hesitated a minute or so. "What did you say?"

"What brought you to this area?" Michael shouted.

"Early retirement. After I sawed off my hand, I was useless. I was using one of them there lumberjack saws, you know the ones that are about five feet long, and have teeth like razors."

"So, the Bull Shark story…it was just…bullshit, right?"

"Yeah, but a lot more exciting. Snorkeling in the keys and being attacked by a giant Bull Shark…I mean if you have to lose a hand… at least you have a thrilling story to tell. Saying my hand was chopped off by a saw in the woods? Ah…how boring! Anyway, it got me the name 'Snork'."

Just then the Snork hit a set of railroad tracks at fifty miles per hour. Michael's rear bounced three feet from the seat.

"Snork! Please take it easy. I hurt my rump yesterday." Michael's death grip on the dashboard handle started to slip and slide.

"Did you fall off a turnip truck or somethin'?"

"Ah, yeah…It happens to me all the time." The Snork laughed. Michael was starting to enjoy Snork's company.

"Listen…if you're going to Jeff's cabin, I was there yesterday," Michael noted. "Ray said Billy was living there. The place reminded me of the Schroon Lake garbage dump!"

"No, I wouldn't go there unless the joint was fumigated. Billy turned it into a rat hole! We're going up to Mt. Defiance. Festus and me…we been livin' up there for the past three months." Michael fondly remembered the many times he and Jeff and his two boys camped up on Mt. Defiance.

"So, you're livin' in the timbers, huh?" Michael asked, feeling it a somewhat naïve question.

"Where the fuck else would we live?"

"A cabin, a tent… what's was wrong with Jeff's place on the lake, before Billy moved in, that is? Oh, never mind!" Michael conceded. It was a moot point since it was clearly too late to consider. "How the hell did you ever get Jeff up the mountain?"

"Mary Jane was the getaway wagon right after I helped him escape from that grubby hospital on a covered gurney. I plunked his ass right in the back. Nobody suspected nothin'. Then I carried him up the mountain fireman's style."

"So that was you I saw in the hallway near his room."

"Yeah. That was me. I saw you but turned my head, so you wouldn't spot me."

"Knew it! You're a damn good friend, Snork! Really, you are! I just don't understand why you didn't make him stay in the hospital and get the medical attention he needed."

Snork smiled and nodded then made a sharp right hand turn on a secluded dirt road. Gravel and dust kicked up and nearly asphyxiated Michael. Attempting to expel the grime from his lungs, he coughed then he held his breath until the air was clear.

"You can't stay up there forever," Michael said still gasping for air. "Maybe it's time to head back to Bridgetown and face the music. Have you been back there lately?"

"Yeah, once. Festus wanted to see his son, Tyler, play in some championship football game. Me and him, we were at the game. I think Tyler saw us. When he flubbed that pass in the end zone causing Bridgetown to blow the game, Festus had a shit fit."

"Why didn't you just stay there and try to work things out with the Chief of Police?"

"With Lefty? You can't be serious! I rather have a hot poker up my ass!"

"Well, I know he's lazy," Michael said. "Word around town has it that for the first time in over 30 years, there is a real chance that Lefty won't be elected again. People are getting really annoyed with him.

He's kissing everyone's ass in town and will arrest anyone just to look good. All he and his deputies do is hang around the station and drink beer all day and…"

"Well, no shit Sherlock," Snork interrupted. "Now, guess I gotta explain the details of why me and Festus…we had to hide out. Hanging in that goddamn hospital ain't safe. With his dipshit brother on the loose up here, I was worried he'd try to slit his throat! In case you didn't know, Billy was the bastard who removed the chocks on the truck wheels causing Festus to fall and nearly 'buy the farm'!"

"Wish we could somehow prove it."

"I don't need fuckin' proof! I just know! Anyway, everyone knows Billy wants his brother dead and will try and find some freakin' way to make it happen! But I'm here to tell you that ain't never gonna as long as I'm around."

Michael shook his head. "Murder his own brother! Damn it's hard to believe."

"Believe it! Ever since they was kids, Billy had a hard-on for Jeff. When Billy beat up Tyler and Jeff found out, he put Billy in the hospital. Remember?"

"Yeah. How could I forget?"

"Ain't no love lost between them two!"

"To make things worse, Ray heard that idiot Lefty wanted to put Festus in the hoosegow for some assault incident up in them there pits he had nothin' to do with. That's when them college kids got attacked. He wasn't even there!"

"You are right, Snork. It was right after Jeff's accident too."

"And listen to this! Then I heard on the radio that Francine was murdered, and Festus was a suspect for that! Maybe we gotta stow away on some freighter to the Far East to be safe! I don't know. So, what's up with that freakin' police chief? Can't that lazy bastard find anyone else to blame? Pretty soon Festus is gonna get blamed for killing John Dillinger!"

Michael sighed. "He's incompetent…pure and simple."

"Oh, I almost forgot. Once that fat cat Igor, the fire boss at the coal mine gets the news about Francine's murder, he'll come a lookin' for Festus too!"

"Look Snork, one problem at a time," Michael said without knowing exactly what he was saying.

"You deal with the 'one problem at a time' thing. Me and my twelve-gauge shotgun… we'll deal with Igor's fat ass just fine!"

"C'mon Snork! That'll just make things ten times worse! Tell me something. Who do you think murdered Francine?"

"It ain't Billy! No goddamn way! He was up here all weekend stayin' in a duck blind across from the cabin. Stayed in it for a couple of days. I'd see the twit at Rays sittin' all by himself for breakfast… all camouflaged up lookin' like a freakin' walking rainforest! I should a wasted him and dumped his body in the garbage dump an give the ole' bears and good old-fashioned feast. Problem is…with that camouflaged suit on… they'd probably think he was a Cesar Salad!" Snork laughed so loud, the Jeep swerved and nearly ended up in a swamp on the side of the road.

"Wait a minute!" Michael said. "Couldn't he have left the area, murdered Francine and returned back the next day? It would have been the perfect alibi."

"Nah, he ain't got enough agates to come up with that one! Billy is two plums short of a fruit pie. He's dumber than dirt."

Snork wheeled his Jeep to the left then up a steep hill. As he made the turn, Michael marveled at the panoramic view of Fort Ticonderoga nestled strategically on Lake Champlain behind him. Lots of memories up here, he said to himself.

They drove another mile until they came to a wooded area only slightly populated with tall pines. Snork veered gradually to the left and found a dirt road about half as wide as the one they were on.

The bright light of the day shown through the tall trees despite their density. The air had a smell of woodland before rain. It is dark for this time of day, so perhaps the filtered light will soon be accompanied by rain.

Michael looked over his right shoulder and noticed the sudsy white ripples of a fast-flowing brook.

"That brook is fed by Schroon Lake and has a thousand trout and salmon in it." Snork noted. Michael quickly understood why Jeff selected this location. The word nirvana came to mind.

After another mile or so, the dirt road disappeared, and they encountered a wall of tall conifers. They could drive no further.

"That's it!" Snork said. "We have to park Mary Jane and hoof it from here."

Snork parked the Jeep at the bottom of a hill and started to walk into the dense forest. Everything was green with no discernable path anywhere that Michael could see. He merely followed the leader.

"I guess you know where the hell you are going. I sure as hell don't."

"Leave everything to me, Mike. This is my home court. Lived in the woods my whole life. It's kind a like your back yard in Bridgetown."

Michael was beyond winded. Every step was pure drudgery. Long tree limbs whipped his face. Small branches and fallen trees laced the ground and obliterated any semblance of a path.

Snork's large body accelerated through the woods as if he were a gazelle.

"Snork! Goddamn it …are you trying to qualify for the Olympics or what? Slow down or you're going to have to give me mouth-to-mouth."

"It's getting late. We gotta get there before Jeff gets tanked!"

"Who the hell cares? Let that numbskull get tanked! I'm getting damn tired of being inconvenienced by Jeff!"

Michael was panting so hard he could barely get the words out. "You have to slow down, Snork!"

"Well, you know Jeff! Every day at three bells he sucks the brew!"

"If we don't slow down soon, I'll be sucking my intestines!"

When they came to a small clearing, Snork found a tree stump and sat down. Michael, on the other hand, taking deep desperate breaths, flung himself to the ground landing on a pile of leaves and a stack of pine needles. He was thoroughly spent.

"I'm going to die!" he wailed.

"We're not too far now," Snork said. "Only about five more miles."

"What! Five more miles? Take me back to Bridgetown. I can't make one more mile!"

"Just come with me." Snork started walking down a small hill. He pulled back a large branch that was camouflaged with foliage. "Look at this," he said.

Between the branches, Michael noticed a small barn-like structure, an improvised shelter that looked like a large garage without any doors. Built with logs, branches, leaves, pine needles, moss, and animal pelts, they are also called Adirondacks (like the mountains) and are quite common all over the highlands. It has a roof and three walls, and the front is left open.

"Can you guess who lives there? Snork asked as he grinned broadly in a smug, mischievous, self-satisfied way.

"A dork named Jeff, maybe?" Michael wasn't smiling

"Don't forget about me! I live there too!"

"Ah, correction then. Snork the dork lives there too! So, are we going to stare at this thing all day or go in and find Davy Crockett?"

"Go right ahead," Snork said as he spread back a bunch of branches. Go right up there. Careful. He might think you are the Fuller Brush Man so call out his name first."

Michael followed a narrow path of trodden leaves and broken twigs for about fifty yards. When he arrived at the shelter, he sat down on a trashed metal cooler and looked around like he was seeing mother earth for the first time. The shelter was about ten feet tall and fifteen feet wide. On the side of the shelter there was an old piece of canvas, perhaps from a dilapidated old Army tent, stretched out to form an extended to the roof.

We have found the hacienda, Michael said to himself. Now where the hell is Sergio?

Snork came up the side, his arms full of kindling wood.

"Ain't nobody home?" he asked.

"Beats the crap out of me," Michael said as he wiped his neck and face with a white hanky.

"He's probably out shootin' cottontails. Stay for the chow Mike! Them gray little bunnies are great eaten!"

"I understand they are quite plentiful up here. But I never cared much for rabbit."

"Yeah, lots a roadkill too! Especially on Rte. 9.

"Hey Mike, you know why rabbits never make no noise when they fuck?"

"Okay, I give." Michael said trying to play along.

"Cause they got cotton balls."

As Snork laughed hysterically, Michael was thinking how totally absurd this expedition into no man's land was but if it produced Jeff, it just might be worth it.

"Cut the crap Snork! Let's go find your playmate, Festus. I need to get back to Bridgetown sometime before the apocalypse!"

"You think you're just gonna walk into them there woods and Festus' gonna pop up like some jack in the box? No way José! Them bears or wolves will get your ass first!"

A frustrated Michael walked over to the shelter and sat down on one of the three bean bag chairs. I'm surprised how comfortable they are, he said to himself as he sank deeply into a chair and heard the sound of the dry beans crunching.

This place was well-furnished, Michael mused. Two sets of bunk beds and a couple chaise lounges, a potbellied stove, and a large ice box were strategically placed in the shelter. When Megan throws me out, at least now I have a place to stay.

Michael closed his eyes and leaned back in the chair and began to ruminate. I have allowed this entire nightmare to get totally out of control. With all that is on my mind: Megan, Francine, Tyler, my financial planning practice on life support… what the hell am I doing sitting here in the middle of the Adirondacks listening to rabbit jokes? I'm not only lost in the mountains, I'm lost in my head. It's almost like the ghost of Francine is contaminating my life! It has wrapped its appendages around me and is devouring me. Yes, I had fallen in love with her but why did I fall so far and so fast? Now that I think about it, my fall was no different than Jeff's. Both have caused considerable damage. And it's going to get worse unless I…well I don't know what. Just then, Michael felt a hand on his shoulder.

"Hey Michael! You old son-of-a-bitch. What's up Dude?"

Michael opened his eyes to the image of Jeff standing directly in front of him holding two rabbits by the ears, one in each hand. A long bow and quiver full of arrows were suspended from his shoulder. Blood dripped on his shoes.

"Could you back off a little," Michael asked with an agitated tone, as tiny puddles of blood pooled on the brown dirt.

"I know how it is. Didn't mean to disturb you, Man, but when I fall asleep in the woods, I'm usually whacked out for about ten hours! Then I wake up in a shitty mood!"

"Goddamn you, Jeff! You've been whacked for the last three months! I'm so pissed at you!" Michael declared angrily "You don't call anyone, you don't let anyone know where you are. You just disappear off the face of the earth. There are some people in your life that care about you – I don't really know why–and you couldn't have cared less! At least you could have let me know where the hell you were. I thought we were friends!"

Jeff laughed dismissively.

"It's not funny, goddamn it!"

"Did you hear the news about what happened to your wife, Francine?"

"Before or after you screwed her?" Jeff laughed again – one of those caustic laughs imbued with a malicious overtone.

Michael was startled by Jeff's comment. While his affections for Francine were still fresh, Michael almost forgot that she was Jeff's wife, at least on paper anyway.

"You're a real son-of-bitch, you know that? Speaking about friends. I thought you were my friend, someone I could trust. Friends don't sleep with their friend's old ladies! How could you stab me in the back like that…of all people?"

"Listen, Jeff! You left her when she needed you most…when she wanted someone to love and care for her. She was a beautiful lady who was a kind and loving person. She had no money and was desperate. She was trying to reform her ways after your brother, Billy, pimped her out and she had to give up Tyler. You stood by and allowed that to happen! Can you imagine how difficult that must have been for her… to give up her son? You were never there, Jeff, so don't try to pretend that you cared. No, Jeff. You're the real son-of-bitch!"

"Just curious. Why did you keep using the word was?" Jeff asked uneasily.

"You didn't know?"

"Didn't know what?"

"My God. You don't know, do you? Francine was murdered." With some sort of selfish retribution, Michael almost relished telling Jeff the news. After all, Jeff should feel the pain of her loss just as he did.

"Murdered! You used the word 'murdered'!" Jeff repeated angrily and loudly. He dropped the rabbits on the ground and ambled to the other bean bag chair dropping his body down hard. "Someone murdered Francine?" he said softly.

Jeff was silent for a few minutes. It took him some time to digest the news. His disposition then changed from rage to remorse and he was overcome with sadness.

"I need to know who did it."

"Well, no one knows for sure but Lefty thinks you or Billy did it."

"Well…Billy's here. Couldn't have been him."

"Here? Where the hell is 'here'?"

"Michael, he had you in his sights and was ready to pull the trigger! You're are one lucky ass Dude. He was perched in my duck blind when you went into my cabin. I jumped him from behind then tied the bastard up and brought him here. Another few seconds and you would have been dead meat. I have him chained up in the woods."

"Chained?"

"Yeah, chained!"

"What are you going to do with him?" Michael asked.

"Black Bear bait? How's that for an alternative? There's also a pack of hungry Timber Wolves roamin' around here killin' the deer. When it happens to Billy, it will be ugly but fast. They go for the jugular first, then they tear off the skin and eat the organs."

"C'mon, Jeff. You not serious."

"Goddamn right, I'm serious!"

"What that bastard did to me and my family…yeah, I'm serious!"

"Snork…did you know about all this?" Michael asked attempting to solicit the voice of reason.

"Tried to talk sense to him," Snork said. "It ain't no use!"

"That's right! It ain't no use! Michael, you know he almost killed me and ruined my family."

Michael was dumfounded to say the least. "So, if an animal doesn't show up, he'll die of dehydration or even malnutrition," he said.

"Oh, don't worry about no animal showing up. We chum that area to attract the animals," Jeff said with a smirk. "We take the garbage out and dump it in the woods right in front of him. It's for the animals in the area but if the asshole really gets hungry, he can eat that!"

"Jeff, you're freakin' delirious!" Jeff's fall a few months ago did affect his thinking. Michael couldn't help remembering Dr. Rheingold warning: if Jeff didn't rest and recover properly, there could be cognitive issues. I can't let this happen!

"You can't do this, Jeff," Michael pleaded. "It's not you. You must stop this insanity! It's first degree murder! Let's take Billy back to Bridgetown and allow the authorities to punish him for what he did to you."

"Now who's delirious? You honestly think anyone in Bridgetown, especially Lefty Margolis, will believe me? How the hell would I prove it?"

"People up here must know the story. I'm sure Billy shot off his mouth to several people about what he did to you. We can get them to testify, right Snork?"

"He told me and Ray, but I don't know who else he told. People up here, they ain't so keen on testifying… they don't like getting involved."

I'm choppin' but the chips aren't flyin'! Michael said to himself. Since common sense wasn't working he decided to try a different approach.

"Jeff what would your mother think if she knew about this? Remember he's your own flesh and blood!"

"He was a bastard to my mother too! I never told you about the time he punched her in the face and knocked out her two front teeth did I."

"No, but knowing Billy, I'm not surprised."

"Or, about the time he stole the family car, took it to the auction and pocketed the money. What kind of scumbag would do that to two elderly people in their eighties?"

"That doesn't surprise me either. But, listen to me! You are putting yourself in the same category as your brother. You're a better a person than he is. Not only that, how will you live with yourself knowing what you had done?"

Jeff listened attentively and after a short interval asked, "So, okay, Michael what would you have me do? Taking him back to Bridgetown would be hopeless."

Michael was encouraged by Jeff's apparent receptiveness but remained unconvinced that he would unshackle Billy.

"Take me to him," he said.

CHAPTER EIGHTEEN

September–1995 – Bridgetown

With a heavy heart Wayne went to work as usual on the Monday morning after Francine's murder. He felt somewhat betrayed by Tyler, feeling sorry for himself employing the after all we've done for him mindset. This is no way to treat us. Molly and I have always been there for him. In fact, you could say we rescued him from a dire situation. Who knows what would have happened to him if he was still living at home with his mother and under Billy's control. When I see him, we are really going to have a heart to heart meeting. This is simply wrong and totally inconsiderate.

The noise at school was vociferous with rampant speculation on who killed Francine. Wayne tried hard to avoid any communication on the subject by hibernating in his office and focusing on the athletic schedule for the coming months. The volleyball and basketball schedules required finalization, not to mention the swimming and wrestling events. As he worked on the December Holiday Wrestling Tournament, he hoped Tyler would participate. He was one of the best wrestlers on the team.

Two days had passed since Tyler's disappearance. Molly couldn't sit still. She was up early and, in her car, driving anxiously around Bridgetown and its outskirts somehow thinking Tyler might magically show up. It was her way of expending nervous energy instead of remaining home and worrying herself sick.

But Molly was troubled by what she considered to be a lack of urgency from the Bridgetown police. The way she saw it, Chief of Police Lefty Margolis had not made a real effort to find Tyler. Therefore, her first stop on her morning odyssey was the police department to speak with the chief directly and find out why.

After she parked her car, Molly walked by four black and white patrol cruisers neatly parked in front of the ruddy brick building that had been the headquarters of the Bridgetown police department for the last seventy years. With Tyler missing, she questioned why they were parked and idle and not out on patrol. That just reconfirms my suspicions about these do-nothing police. She could feel the built up of wrath in her belly and tried hard to calm herself down before she entered the building.

She walked down a dark hallway until she came to a door that had a sign that said Bridgetown Police Department. She had to push hard to open it, as if it was purposely difficult in order to ward off unwanted visitors, especially female ones.

"Hello," she said to the receptionist. "I'm Molly Winslow and I would like to speak with Chief Margolis."

"Oh!" said the receptionist, as if she was surprised by Molly's visit. Heather Newman sat behind a small rectangular table next to a telephone and an antiquated Smith Corona. Molly felt her worn-out jeans and old sweatshirt were unbecoming for a public employee.

"Chief Margolis is in a very important meeting," she said. "Do you have an appointment?"

"No"

"Well…okay. But he usually works by appointment only. I'll make an exception this time but next time we will expect you to call first."

"Okay," Molly responded gritting her teeth forcing herself to maintain control.

"You'll just have to wait."

"How long?" Molly asked.

"Mrs. Winslow, I said he's dealing with some very significant issues."

"Thank you," Molly said. She thought to herself, Yeah sure. He's probably taking a nap. Molly took a seat on the dilapidated wooden chair in the so-called reception area.

As she sat down, she could hear the good ole' boy banter coming from the chief's office. Molly felt the snub and obvious brush off by the receptionist and was angry.

Guess I have no choice but to sit here until the chief finishes his morning bullshit session with his posse. After thirty minutes of waiting respectfully, she rose from her chair and marched bravely right into the chief's office.

"Would you mind explaining to me why I have to wait so long to speak with you?" she said, as she stood erect with her hands gripping her hips.

The chief, who was leaning against his front desk chomping on his proverbial cigar with an open can of beer in his hand, immediately changed his expression from casual to stern.

"Excuse me!" Molly declared. "Is this some sort of policemen's shindig or what? I shouldn't have to remind you, gentleman, that my foster son, Tyler, is still missing while you sit here on your butts drinking booze and shooting BS!"

Two deputies, Thomas Prescott and Ralph Williams, seated in the arm chairs, their ties casually loosened, laughing, kibitzing, with an open bottle of Jim Beam on the table, their shot glasses full, bounded over their chairs and evacuated the room. As they left, they quickly fixed their ties, tucked in their shirts, and looked like they had seen Frankenstein's monster.

"Mrs. Winslow, you just can't barge in here like this!" This is a reputable law enforcement office," the chief exclaimed. "We have rules!"

Yeah, Molly thought. About as reputable as Bubba's Horse Room down the street! "When it comes to finding my boy, Tyler, I assure you, I can barge into anyplace I want!"

"Have you filed a missing person's report?" the chief asked.

"Go to hell! You know what you can do with your 'missing person's report'. Tyler has been missing for three days and you know it!"

"Look! Mrs. Winslow, we need that ten-step report!"

"This police department is pathetic!" Molly blurted. "You ought to be damned ashamed of yourself! I'll find Tyler myself and the first place I am checking is the sand pits – where you should have checked yourself!"

The chief walked toward her in a futile effort to implore her understanding. "Mrs. Winslow…please! There are some very dangerous people lurking in this town. I urge you to reconsider. Trying to locate Tyler yourself would be very unsafe."

"Well then, let me tell you this Mr. Chief of Police. If anything happens to me, it will be on your fat ass." Molly stormed out of the chief's office, bounded into her car, and drove off in a huff. An intense burning sensation was rising in her. *That goddamn lazy bastard isn't going to tell me what to do!*

Lefty walked out to the reception area where Thomas Prescott was flirting with the receptionist. "Thomas!" Lefty yelled. "I hate to interrupt your extra-curricular time, but I want you to keep an eye on Mrs. Walden and make sure she doesn't get into trouble."

"Okay Chief," Thomas replied. "I'm on her like white on rice!" Lefty laughed at Thomas's unfortunate choice of words.

Molly drove a few miles from town, pulled over to the side of the road, and started to cry.

"Tyler, Honey, where in God's name are you?"

She leaned her head back on the bolster, lifted the seat recliner lever up, laid back, closed her eyes, and prayed. As she examined her options, she remembered stories of the Romano Sand Pits, how so many Bridgetown kids would go up there to play and even hide when they didn't want to go home. *I think I'll just to go up there and drive around a little – see what's going on.*

The long dusty dirt road at the east end of the sand pits was blocked at the entrance with two red A-frame barricades. Warning signs to prevent intrusion were nonexistent except for an old dilapidated do not trespass sign hanging from a nearby tree.

Molly simply ignored the sign and drove around the barricades proceeding up the hill into a wooded area where wild brush and tall grass replaced the dirt road. A cluster of small trees stopped her forward movement, at least until she figured out a way to circumvent them. She backed up, selected another pathway and continued onward into an open area of flat grass and small precipices.

Molly could see several yellow earthmoving vehicles: diggers, excavators, dumpers and bulldozers working up on a nearby hill extracting rock and aggregate from the ground and loading dumper trucks to transport the materials to local concrete plants.

I should probably leave, she said to herself. She surveyed the area. If I must, I can get back to the car fast.

When she opened the car door, a strange unprotected feeling engulfed her. She walked gingerly, as if one wrong footstep might set off an alarm. Suddenly, she became frightened. Was that twigs breaking under someone's feet? No one would ever find me up here she said to herself. Maybe I should get back to the car, lock myself inside and see if I can navigate out of this place.

The breaking twigs became louder. She knew someone was near. "Tyler is that you?" she shouted. Whomever it was didn't answer. That frightened her even more.

She started to run towards her car and tripped on an outstretched tree limb. As she rose, she felt a pair of very strong arms clutch her from behind. She couldn't see her assailant and started to scream.

"You can scream all you want, bitch! Nobody's going to hear you up here!" She felt a hard blow to her head and collapsed on the ground unconscious.

CHAPTER NINETEEN

September – 1995 – Mt. Defiance

"**B**illy is tied to the large tree on the other side of a swamp. It's an hour hike from here," Jeff said. There's a poncho and an extra pair of goulashes in the shelter for you to use – if you want them."

Michael looked at his watch. "It's 1:30 p.m.," he noted. "Will we get back before dark? This is last place on earth I want to be when it gets the dark!"

"Of course!" Jeff replied spontaneously. "You stay here and guard the 'station', okay Snork?"

"You got it, boss man."

"Do you have a walkie-talkie?" Michael asked

"Shit no! Who the hell needs a walkie-talkie. They're for greenhorns! I have my compass and flashlight just in case."

"Just in case of what?" Michael asked.

"In case it gets dark. What else would we need a flashlight for?"

"Thought you said we'd be back before dark?"

"I did! But you never know – unpredictable things happen all the time in the woods."

"Why did you put him so far away?" Michael asked, as they started to walk through the brush.

"I didn't want anyone to find the scumbag. It's that simple."

Michael still had difficulty wrapping his head around what Jeff did to his brother. Something in the recesses of his mind told him Jeff is not acting like his normal self. I need to watch him closely.

After a few hundred yards their progress slowed. They were pushing branches away from their faces, their feet were sinking into the spongy earth. The wind started to gust, and trees swayed precipitously above them. Rain was in the air. Soon lightning started to flash in the sky.

"Jeff! Slow down, goddamn it!" Michael's Poncho was too large, his goulashes too small, and his frame of mind too negative. He could already feel the blisters forming on his feet. And there was nothing more he hated than blisters.

"We have to make time before we get caught in a thunder storm so crank up your ass, Michael! We gotta get movin'!"

It seemed like every branch in the forest whipped at Michael's face as he moved, and he had to use his hands to keep them away. He felt like he was heading into a deep black hole in the woods and would be lost forever. With every few steps, he felt more irrelevant to the world almost as if he was on another planet.

"Michael, there's a shelter ahead. We can stop for a few minutes, so you can catch your breath."

Turns out the so-called shelter was a bunch of standing trees growing closely together. Michael was panting hard. He couldn't wait to sit on a stump in the middle of the bushes under the trees. It started to rain hard. Rotted trees lay strewn across the ground.

"How much farther," Michael asked.

"Far!" Jeff said curtly.

"You sound pissed at me."

"To tell you the truth, I am very pissed off at you. How could you sleep with my woman?"

"Are you going to chain me up to a tree too?"

"I really did love her, you know." Jeff said as he lit up a cigarette and leaned against a tree.

"I did too." Michael admitted. "I did too."

"But, you should know, Jeff, she was trying hard to get her act together. She had a job at the bakery and a restraining order against Billy. She was planning on taking courses to become a financial planning assistant. In fact, I was going to help her out financially and then hire her after she completed her courses. So, our relationship was much more than a one-night stand."

"What about my son, Tyler?"

"Tyler is what motivated her to shape up her life. She wanted to regain custody of him."

"That upsets me so much!" Jeff said. He stared at the ground scornfully.

"What upsets you so much?"

"Tyler being in a foster home! He's my son and I wanted custody, but Francine screwed me!"

"Keep in mind, Jeff, Social Services is trying to do the right thing. With you working up here in Schroon Lake all the time, and Francine on drugs and under Billy's control, what kind of life was that for Tyler? What would you describe as the right thing for Tyler?"

"He should be with me, goddamn it!"

"I'll tell you the same thing I told Francine. That's entirely up to you. Prove to Social Services that you can handle the responsibilities of fatherhood and I'm sure you could gain custody of Tyler."

"Will you help me?"

"Jeff, for crying out loud! You know I will!"

Jeff inhaled a final drag on his cigarette and threw it on the ground crushing it with his foot until it was thoroughly pulverized.

"I appreciate that very much, Michael. I really love that kid a lot."

"I know you do, Jeff."

"I have lived an irresponsible life. I had no business hurting Francine and Tyler like I did. I was selfish and inconsiderate. I want to make amends for Tyler's sake. I have some money saved. I want the best for Tyler."

"It's not too late," Michael noted.

Jeff contemplated for a few moments then said, "I shot my first deer right over there–near that cluster of shrubs. I always knew what all hunters knew—footprints, droppings, broken branches indicating a trail a deer might have followed. Wish I knew as much about raising a family."

"Just for the hell of it, how do you explain your success as a hunter and fisherman?" Michael asked curiously.

"When hunting, I try to think like a deer. When fishing I try to think like a fish!"

Michael didn't pursue it further but wondered how a person could think like a deer and fish. What the hell did deer and fish think about other than eating, surviving, and screwing? He didn't doubt the veracity of Jeff's answer and finally concluded that Jeff possessed a special predisposition for hunting and fishing and leave it at that. Call it instinctual.

A gust of wind and a crack of thunder interrupted their brief interlude, but Michael was pleased with his candid conversation with Jeff.

"We'd better get our asses in gear!" Jeff said. "There is one helluva storm coming!"

Chapter Twenty

September–1995 Highland Hospital – Bridgetown

Molly opened her eyes slowly. Her head was throbbing like a time bomb. Her blurred vison obscured the tall figure standing at the far end of the dark room. She kept asking herself, where am I? Who is this person? Why did he hurt me?

The figure moved slowly toward her. She became more anxious. She covered her eyes with the palms of her hands. What seemed like an eternity was only a few seconds, but Molly was so frightened she had lost track of time.

"Molly, it's me." A voice said softy. "We're in the hospital."

Still trembling from being accosted, Molly was disoriented and scared. She wanted to respond but was too choked up to say anything. All she could do was quietly sob.

"Molly…don't be afraid. I'm here and I'll take care of you."

She breathed deeply and regained some composure. "Tyler, honey. Is it really you?"

"Yes, it really is. How do you feel?" He pulled the covers up closer to her chin and patted her arm tenderly, then placed an ice pack under her head. He sat down on the bed near her feet.

"My head is exploding. What happened to me?"

"I'm not sure exactly but I was walking on the road to go home when I heard loud screams. When I ran to you, I saw someone running away. You were unconscious. I picked you up and began walking out of the pits. When I got to the bottom of the hill, an ambulance was pulling in. It parked right next to an empty police cruiser."

"I'm glad you called the ambulance, Tyler."

"I didn't. I don't have a phone."

"Somebody did. Ambulances don't just show up unannounced."

"What about the empty cop car?" Tyler asked.

"This is a real mystery. They are so derelict in that department, they disappear into thin air!"

"I know. Wayne said that Chief Margolis doesn't know his ass from his elbow."

"Tyler! Your language!

"Oops, sorry."

"So, you didn't you see the person that ran away?"

"No. But the ambulance guys…they examined you and decided to take you to emergency. I rode with them. The doctors were in a few minutes ago and said you had a slight concussion. They want to keep you here overnight for observation. I called Wayne. He's on his way."

"For God's sake, Tyler, where've you been? We've been beyond distressed! You just can't leave like that!"

Tyler could feel Molly's mixed emotions. He knew she was upset but also relieved he was safe. He felt secure and grateful recognizing how lucky he was to have people like Molly and Wayne in his life.

"I'm sorry. I've been camping out in the woods near the sand pits. I was embarrassed to come home. After I dropped that pass and lost the game for Bridgetown, I couldn't face you and Wayne. It was wrong. I was inconsiderate."

"Come here," Molly appealed. She reached up as Tyler bent over and they hugged each other. "I was so worried about you. Don't ever go away again without telling us where you are!"

Unexpectedly, another fear gripped Molly. As she hugged Tyler, she realized he needed to be told about his mother's murder. But she was afraid. Breaking the news to him right now seemed inappropriate given all that she had been through. She didn't have the energy or emotional wherewithal to deal with a matter so distressing. I'll wait for Wayne and we'll share the bad news with Tyler together.

CHAPTER TWENTY-ONE

September – 1995 – Mt. Defiance

It was 3:30 p.m. and very stormy. Slogging through the mud, rain, and cold for the last hour was a lot worse than Michael anticipated. He never realized how much raindrops could sting when the wind gusted.

They were getting closer to Billy. The pungent stench of rotting garbage was a disgusting clue. "Smells like rotten eggs, doesn't it?" Jeff noted.

"Well, it sure as hell doesn't smell like Chanel Number Five, does it?"

"For sure!" Jeff conceded.

"Wait!" Michael said. "Let's talk."

"Okay." Jeff lit up a Marlboro.

"When we get there, what will we do with him?" Michael asked.

"I guess we have no other choice other than do what you said. Let's take him to back to Bridgetown."

"Good. Jeff, you know it's the right thing to do."

"I'd really like to let the bears and wolves have at 'em!"

Michael decided not to respond. He was determined not to allow Jeff to follow through with his original solution and was glad he came around to his way of thinking – no matter how reluctant he was.

At the same time, he really couldn't disagree with Jeff. Lefty Margolis has had Jeff and Billy on his radar screen (shit list) for quite some time and would probably arrest them the minute they showed up in Bridgetown. What worried Michael most, is that Lefty would manufacture some trumped up evidence and have them both sent to the Attica Correctional Facility for a very long time. Billy deserves it. Jeff doesn't. By the same token, Billy doesn't deserve to be cannibalized by wild animals either!

They continued their trudge through the wild. After another twenty minutes they came upon a swamp the size of a gymnasium.

"Over there near the end of the swamp," Jeff pointed. "See him? I chained the bastard to an Almanack Red Spruce. It is the strongest tree in the Adirondacks! It's also called the Queen of the Adirondacks! Nothing but the best for my miserable brother!"

"Follow me!" Jeff ordered. He began walking around the perimeter of the swamp leading to where Billy was chained. As they approached that area, the odor became so intense, Michael took out his handkerchief to cover his mouth and nose.

Seeing Billy behind the pile of toxic garbage was more than difficult; it was repulsive. Michael got a better view as he walked around the pile.

"Don't get too close!" Jeff shouted.

In addition to a fifteen-foot snow tire chain wrapped around him like a steel blanket, handcuffs were tightly secured to the chain immobilizing his arms completely. Manacles bit into his ankles. His wrists and ankles were swollen, cut and bleeding. Blood was flowing profusely from his mouth as if someone pulverized his face with a piece of timber – and – Jeff probably did. Overwhelmed by the weight of the chain alone, Billy was hunched over like a gorilla on life support.

"Got 'em giftwrapped pretty good, huh?" Jeff boasted as if Billy was some kind of sacrificial gift to the gods. Whatever primeval curse had come over Jeff to do such a thing, Michael knew he had to stop it. This is insane!

"Jeff, I can't tell you how sadistic this is! This is not you!"

"Did you forget, Michael? A few days ago, you were a split second away from having your head blown off by this animal."

Not saying a word, Billy looked up at Michael with the most venomous expression he had ever seen. He knew if Billy could get his hands on him he would tear him from limb to limb.

Michael's brain was racing. Jeff was in no mood for compassion, that was for sure. He started to walk to the other side of Billy to get a better look at the chain configuration. Billy's eyes followed Michael's every move.

"Michael! Stay back!" Jeff reminded him again and again.

Just then, Billy vaulted from the ground with his arms extended as far as they could go, and when he came down he had them around Michael's neck. Michael screamed with pain. He felt like his head was trapped between the jaws of a iron clamp. Steel cuffs on Billy's arms burrowed into his collar bones. Billy's huge biceps bulged as he gripped Michael so tightly, he was beginning to lose consciousness.

Billy screamed, "Unlock the fucken chains, you bastard! Unlock them now or I'll kill 'em!"

Sheer horror overwhelmed Jeff. He knew unless Michael was released from the stranglehold Billy had on him, he would surely asphyxiate. Jeff had no choice. He reached for the keys in his pocket then unlocked the collar padlock.

When Michael and the chain dropped to the ground, Billy hurdled over them and tackled Jeff to the ground. With Jeff flat on his back, Billy thrusted his knee into his chest and began pummeling his face viciously. Michael managed to get up and grab Billy's shirt collar and yank him off Jeff.

"You're a dead man!" Billy shouted as he found a log the size of a baseball bat.

"I'm gonna tear your head off and shit down your neck, you mother fucken bastard!" Michael put his hands up to defend himself. He knew he was no match for Billy. But Billy pursued him and the closer he got, the more Michael concluded this was his swan song, his grand finale. This is how my life will end.

Billy swung the log at Michael's face but missed as Michael lunged at his feet and knocked him down. Billy dropped hard into a deep trench of mud near the swamp hitting his head on a rock knocking him out. Michael helped Jeff to his feet. His face was bloodied but he had enough strength in his legs to walk.

"C'mon Jeff! Let's get the fuck out of here!" Michael screeched.

They followed the same path they used to get there.

"Faster, Jeff! Billy is getting up! We've got to move our asses!" In his condition, Jeff could only run so fast and Billy was gaining on them.

"Wait a goddamn minute! We ain't gonna make it!" Jeff exclaimed.

Michael got down on one knee to rest. Jeff reached into his pocket and pulled out his pistol. As much as Michael opposed Jeff shooting Billy, at this point he knew it was either him or them. Now Michael would be more than happy to pull the trigger himself.

Billy was about fifty yards behind them. Jeff fired one shot and missed. He gripped the gun tightly with both hands aligning the front and back sights. His feet were planted firmly on the ground and pointed in the direction of his target.

Just as he was about to squeeze the trigger, two grizzled Timber Wolves darted from the bush, each weighing nearly 150 pounds. One attacked Billy high–above the shoulders, the other attacked him low– at his feet. Once they had him on his back they gnawed viciously at his throat.

"Shoot them!" Michael screamed. "Shoot them!"

"It's too late! Billy's a goner! If I shoot and wound one of them they will track us down! Usually when there are one or two there's pack of ten.

"C'mon! Let's get the hell out of here!"

They ran as fast as they could in the direction from which they came and hoped and prayed that the wolves didn't follow them.

CHAPTER TWENTY-TWO

September–1995–Bridgetown

Several hours had elapsed since Police Chief Lefty Margolis ordered Thomas Prescott, one of his deputies, to follow Molly Winslow as she searched for her foster son, Tyler. When Thomas returned, he went directly into his cubicle, and began filling out a police report. It was straightforward. I followed Molly to the sandpits, waited at the entrance, when she didn't return, I called the ambulance.

Meanwhile, Lefty relaxed in his office. He lit up a cigar, leaned back in his chair, and placed his feet up on his desk. He derived great pleasure looking at his specially ordered police boots. He would only wear Frye Engineer Boots with a gold buckle on the side and his initials etched in gold on the heels.

There was a lot of gold in Lefty's life. His teeth, his badges, the trim on his gun holster, his awards were all in gold. When he received an award, he would always remove the wooden frame and buy a gold frame instead. A picture of Lefty on the cover of Life Magazine framed in gold was on his credenza. But Lefty was never on the cover of Life Magazine.

Thomas Prescott walked into Lefty's office, handed him his police report, and then sat down on the cushiony couch in the middle of the office. He was so tall and lanky; when he sat down and folded his knees, they almost obscured his face and made it nearly impossible to get up again.

Lefty reached for the bottle on Jim Beam on his desk and poured himself a full glass.

"A little Jimmy B on the rocks, Thomas?" Lefty asked.

"Shit yes!" Thomas agreed.

"Go ahead… pour yourself your own goddamn glass. The ice is in the fridge."

"Can you imagine…that bitch barging into my office and interrupting our meeting? And the way she talked to me…let me tell you…for a woman, she's got a lot of balls!"

Lefty read Thomas's police report. "Just curious. Why didn't you follow her into the pits?"

"She just up and vanished and I ain't never been up there before."

"Oh? There is only one path into the pits," Lefty noted.

"I couldn't find no path. Finally, I went on over and had a tall one with one of them there construction workers."

"I don't blame you. Why risk your ass for that foul-mouthed bitch?"

"Did anyone find her?" Thomas asked.

"You called the ambulance, right?"

"Yup. Didn't want to take no chances."

"Looks like the kid…what's his name… Tyler found her. She's in the hospital now."

"Why is that?"

"Supposedly, somebody clocked her on the head, probably one of them construction workers trying to get laid. Guess she's got a concussion. Tyler found her before the construction worker had a chance to drop his drawers. Too bad!"

"Yeah, she really needs a good fuck," Thomas said.

"Any leads yet on who wasted Francine?" Thomas asked. "My money is on that Jeff Walden character…he did it for sure."

"You think he'd murder his own wife?" Lefty asked with a surprised tone.

"Yeah. After she pissed him off by sleeping with everyone in town except the school librarian…yeah, I think he did it."

"She's been trying hard to turn over a new leaf, you know. She developed a connection with Michael Alexander. Did you know that?"

Thomas sniggered. "They had a connection, alright and it was about yay long!" Thomas measured with his two hands about a foot apart.

"Ralph's been poking around all over town. I'll see what he has uncovered later."

"Well, Chief. I don't think Ralph could find his pecker if it was attached to his nose. Look, I don't want to bash the guy, but he really does have shit for brains. He told me one of them Mexican guys working up in them pits was his buddy. He said his name was Manual Labor. Do you believe that?"

Lefty laughed "C'mon Thomas, he's just pullin' your chain!"

"Yeah? What chain is that?" Thomas asked.

And he says Ralph has shit for brains. Lefty was still laughing as he stood up. It was his signal to Thomas that the meeting was over, and he should leave.

"Go find someone we can hang this shit on. Murders, assault, and rape…what the fuck is this town coming to?"

CHAPTER TWENTY-THREE

September – 1995 – The Trip Home

It was midnight. The rain had passed but the sky was still dark and foreboding. Traffic was light at this hour as Jeff and Michael advanced in a southerly direction on Route 87 towards Albany. They were still traumatized. They both knew they would never forget their horrific experience on Mt. Defiance.

But, so far, their trip back to Bridgewater had been uncharacteristically silent, void of their usual back and forth banter. Michael initiated conversation with Jeff but all he could elicit from Jeff were one-word responses. It wasn't until they reached Utica that Jeff opened up.

"You know, Michael, I'm not proud of the way I have behaved with Francine and especially with Tyler. I will always feel responsible for her death, just as if I stabbed her to death myself." Jeff started to tear up. "I can see how you could have fallen so deeply for her. You were right, Michael. I abandoned her and allowed Billy to abuse her. She really didn't have a choice and I should have known that!"

"It takes a man to admit when he is wrong, Jeff."

"If I had it to do over again, I would have studied hard in high school and gone to college. I've always wanted to become a Forest Ranger. It's too late now."

"Jeff, you are still a rather young guy. You have time on your side."

"I just don't have the temperament for school – never did."

"Well, that's for you to decide – I mean – if you want it badly enough you will figure out a way to get it."

"Yeah, I guess…so far I've pretty much wasted my life. I don't want the second half of my life to be like the first half."

"Something to think about."

"Oh, yeah. I am thinking about it – that's for sure."

"Hey listen, Jeff. I'm sorry about Francine. I never should have allowed myself to get involved with her."

"That makes two of us," Jeff smiled. "Forget about it. Just help me with Tyler."

"I am sorry though."

"Please Michael. Do me a favor and don't talk about it."

Michael sensed Jeff's pain. It reminded him of his own pain. Strangely, because of their shared grief, Michael felt closer to Jeff than he ever had before.

"Do you think Snork will keep his promise?" Michael asked.

"He knows I'll kick his ass from here to Sunday if he opens his fat trap to anyone."

"Well, if he does, he'll be implicated too."

"Nah. We're good," Jeff said confidently.

"Hope you're right, Jeff. If we ever piss him off, he has us by the short hairs."

"Listen Michael, drop me off at Monroe's. I want to stay away from my parents for a while. I know I'm going to have to tell them, sooner or later. Maybe they won't even give a rat's ass anyway. Billy hasn't seen them in years."

"Do you think anyone will ever find him…I mean what's left of him?"

"Nope," Jeff quickly replied. "When them wolves get done with him, whatever is left will be devoured by them Turkey Vultures bones and all. Them freakin' scavengers… they'll gorge themselves until there ain't nothin' left."

"Jeff, how old are your parents?"

"Old! Dad is 84, Mom is 82."

"Are you sure you want them to know?"

"What do you mean?"

"Assuming Billy was still alive, if your parents never saw him again, would you be surprised?"

"No."

"Would your parents be surprised?"

"No. They'd probably be grateful!"

"Then why put them through the agony of telling them their son was gored to death by two wolves? Just let them live the rest of their lives in peace."

"You mean… don't tell them?" Jeff eyes filled with tears and he sniffled.

"That's up to you. I'm just asking some questions."

"Right now, Michael, all I want to do is get a good night's sleep and forget all about what the hell happened today!"

After Michael dropped Jeff off at Monroe's house, he headed for his home. His thoughts rapidly transitioned from Jeff, his parents, and Mt. Defiance to how he would explain his sudden departure to Megan.

I've got a lot of work to do he said to himself. I just hope Megan and the kids will forgive me. The thought of facing them made him nauseous. He could hear the rumble of acids converging deep in his abdomen. I haven't eaten in two days. Then again, I'm sure I couldn't keep any food down anyway.

As Michael pulled in the driveway, he was surprised when nothing happened when he pushed the remote garage door opener button. Batteries must be dead. The front door was locked, and his key didn't fit. What the hell? Megan had to be home. Her car is in the driveway. He rang the doorbell at least ten times. Then he pounded on the front window. How could she be so forgetful as to lock me out?

He walked to the side of the garage door and entered the garage code manually on the keypad. When he walked in, he found everything he owned – his clothes, computers, stereo equipment, books – piled neatly in the far corner of the garage. A sealed envelope with his name on it rested on to top of the books. He opened it carefully and read the note inside.

Dear Michael,

I have been trying to figure out where we go from here. Needless to say, Michael, you have broken my heart. We had such a good life. My disappointment in you runs deep. I am angry and severely hurt. Any option that includes our continuing to live together is totally unacceptable to me. You have violated my trust and I can never forgive you for that.

Just so you know, I spoke with Morris Kaplan yesterday and asked him to draw up divorce papers. Let me know where you are staying, and I'll have him forward them to you.

Megan

Michael folded the letter, placed it back in the envelope. Then he walked back to his car, sat in the front seat and he began to cry.

CHAPTER TWENTY-FOUR

September – 1995–Bridgetown

Black H1 Hummer 4-door wagons were an uncommon sight on the streets of Bridgetown. So, when one rolled down main street and parked in front of Luigi's, it was quite a spectacle. Enhancing its sinister appearance was the sticker on the rear bumper. It had the skull and crossbones on it and read coal miner with an attitude in bold black letters.

Chief Lefty Margolis usually enjoyed his morning breakfast each day at Luigi's, where the Bridgetown cognoscenti gathered to resolve the pressing issues of the day. Amid sounds of an antique juke box playing Luigi's favorite tunes from the fifties, there was always a spirited debate in progress.

Lefty always took the middle spot at the counter, on a red swivel stool, a prime ringside seat at the deli. Ollie Smith, owner of a small potato farm outside of town, was always seated on the stool next to him and always had something to add to every conversation.

But this was Lefty's bully pulpit. After all, he was a prominent public official who had a right to expound his views in a public forum.

"How are you this lovely morning, Handsome?" Betty, the waitress asked.

"Good. A cup a java, four eggs over easy with bacon."

"Right away, Chief."

As Lefty read the morning paper, someone selected Bring Back that Lovin' Feeling by the Righteous Brothers on the juke box.

Ollie Smith started to lip-sync the words:

> Bring back that lovin' feelin'
> Whoa, that lovin' feelin'
> Bring back that lovin' feelin'
> 'Cause it's gone, gone, gone.

"For Christ's sake, Ollie. Shut the fuck up will you!"

The headlines were still fresh. It was three days since Francine's murder and the deli was abuzz with speculation. Who did it? Why? Were the rumors about Michael Alexander true?

"Hey Chief, when are you going arrest Jeff Walden?" a customer prodded.

"Yeah," someone else shouted. "The bastard is guilty as shit!"

"I think you should arrest Michael Alexander! His donut was in her coffee!"

Lefty swiveled on his stool and said, "Look everyone, like I've always said, everyone is a suspect, yet no one is a suspect."

"C'mon Lefty! What the hell does that mean?"

"It means he ain't got no fuckin' idea who done it," someone hollered with a gruff voice from the back of the deli. After he made the remark, he walked slowly toward the front of the deli. Lefty was daunted by the sheer size of the man and the blatant anger in his eyes.

Placing his enraged face in front of Lefty's, he said, "I'm here to tell you that if you ain't got a clue real soon, I'm gonna waste 'em both! And, as for you, how 'bout I put a bullet in your brain? Probably will double your I.Q. don't you think?" The man laughed hysterically and then was attacked by a coughing spell as he walked out of the deli.

"Who the fuck was that?" Lefty asked.

Ollie started to hum, I want to be around to pick up the pieces. A stark silence engulfed the deli. "You don't want to mess with that Dude, that's for sure," whispered Ollie."

"Ollie! I thought I told you to shut the fuck up?"

"No one's above the law!" Lefty said indignantly. "I'm the law in this town and no one is going to run ruff shod over it!" He got up abruptly from his stool and left the deli.

"Don't you want your eggs and bacon?" Betty shouted as he stormed out.

"Forget the goddamn order!" Lefty said angrily.

"I'll have them," Ollie said sheepishly.

Betty laughed and obeyed. "You know, Ollie, you are the best garbage can I have in this joint!"

When Lefty arrived at his office, the same man was slouched ill-manneredly on his couch pruning his fungus riddled fingernails with a switchblade. Fingernail scum collected into a small disgusting mound on his belly. A glass of Jim Beam was on the table next him.

"Do you mind?" Lefty asked curtly. This is my office!"

"Yeah, as a matter of fact I do mind! Go ahead! Arrest me for clipping my finger nails."

"How did you get in here? My door is always locked, and the receptionist doesn't come in til ten."

"That's for me to know and you to find out."

Looking at the man, Lefty couldn't help but reconsider his approach. At 6'5" and 300 lbs., this guy had specially made steel toed muck boots to hold up his enormous frame. Adding to his scraggly shoulder length black hair he had a surplus of bedraggled facial hair so plentiful it nearly concealed his mouth.

He was an intimidating figure to say the least and Lefty was smart enough to keep his distance. Given his size and temperament, Lefty could picture himself being crushed like a bug. I'll wait until my deputies get here and then deal with him, he thought. But the man was in no mood to wait for anything.

"I prefer Chivas but this shit ain't all that bad," he said as he took a big gulp of Lefty's Jim Beam then wiped his mouth with his forearm.

"Who the hell are you, anyway?"

"My name is Igor. Igor Gunderson. And I'll be your worst nightmare if you don't get your ass in gear! Name sound familiar?"

"Can't say that it does," Lefty replied.

"Well, isn't that wonderful! The long arm of the law ain't that long here in Bridgeport or Bridgetown or whatever the fuck the name of this sorry ass burg is. Francine is, or should I say was my daughter until someone slaughtered her in your town!"

Igor sniffled then groaned and started to weep. "Someone's gonna pay, goddamn it!" He wiped his eyes with his red and white spotted hanky. Then he blew his nose with a cacophony that almost brought the building down.

"Sorry about that, but I knew her as Francine Walden, Jeff Walden's wife."

"You know what I think?" Igor asked.

"No. tell me."

"I think you don't know jack shit!"

"Look, we ain't got no evidence yet." Lefty said.

"Go get it or I'll get it for you!

"My deputies and me… we've been workin' round the clock on this," Lefty said.

"Deputize me! I have balls the size of quail eggs! I'll make the goddamn problem go away so fast you'll look like a goddamn rock star in this town. I'll be the prosecutor and executioner all in one badass son-of-a bitch. And no one will know nothin'!"

"Deputize you? Is that what you said?"

"You got horse shit in them ears or what? Yeah! Deputize me! I'll find the bastard who killed my daughter…you can bet your sweet flabby ass I will!"

Despite Igor's boorish nature, Lefty envisioned an opportunity. Igor could do the dirty work; the pick and shovel work that Lefty hated to do. If people thought this case was solved (even if it really wasn't)– it would help my chances for re-election.

"Do your deputies have any brains or are they stupid like you?" Igor asked.

"Listen…You should show me some respect. I been Chief of Police here for thirty years and developed a fine reputation for enforcing the law! I expect more appreciation from you!"

"Appreciation, my ass! I think you're a goddamn joke! Look at you! You're a slob! I'm a slob too but I'm not posing as the Chief of Police. You're worthless. All you do is sop up booze all day! This case should have been solved days ago! You're nothing but a hind end around here!"

"Anyway... listen to me, Officer Dipshit. One of your deputies …if you can find one with balls and brains…. I know that's a rare combination around here…assign him to me."

"Okay. You can work with Thomas Prescott."

"Correction! He will work for me not with me."

"Okay, we have a deal." Lefty said. "Now, raise your right hand."

Just give me the fuckin' badge. I ain't takin' no goddamn oath! Don't mean squat in this shithole of a town anyway!"

Lefty attempted to pin the badge on Igor's shirt. "Just want you to know the last moron that tried to pin something on me stabbed my nipple. He's under a pile of firewood back in Morgantown."

"On second thought, I'll just hand it to you."

"Oh, by the way…where are those bastards now?"

"What 'bastards' are you referring to?"

"Festus Walden and Michael Alexander that's who! The dudes that wasted my daughter! Back in Morgantown, they call me 'The Enforcer'. You want to know why?"

"Not really." Lefty said awkwardly. At this point he wished Igor would just go away.

"I warned that Festus creep a long time ago that if anything ever happened to my Francine, his naked carcass would be dropped under the electric coal cutter…the one that undercuts coal and drops it on a conveyer belt. It's fifteen feet high and has sharp teeth five feet long. I told him to picture his body parts on this conveyer belt rolling beside hunks of coal. Get my drift Chief Asshole?"

Lefty was almost speechless. "But we are not sure they killed your daughter, he stammered. "I thought you were going do some investigating first?"

"Hey, numb nuts, listen to me… you want this problem to go away or not?"

Lefty started to think. Walden and Alexander have been a pain in my ass for the last ten years and a menace to society. This would be an excellent opportunity to get rid of the son-of-a bitches permanently… whether they are guilty of killing Francine of not.

CHAPTER TWENTY-FIVE

September – 1995 – Railroad Tracks–Bridgetown

The grief Tyler felt over his mother's murder was growing. He needed time–time to think – time to sort out the facts. Gnawing questions of who killed her and why she was killed were ravaging his mind. He decided to return to his old home on Market Street where his mother was so brutally murdered. Perhaps he could find some clues.

Unwilling to penetrate the bright yellow police barricade tape surrounding the house, Tyler walked across the street to the railroad tracks and began walking on them, one railroad tie at a time.

Autumn foliage bordered both sides of the rails. Thin carpets of leaves blended to create warm shades of yellow, red, and russet over the steely gray stones on either side of the tracks. The spaces between the nine-foot-long railroad ties were choked with weeds.

Tyler was bothered by a pungent aroma. The day long sun had softened the creosote on the railroad ties creating a familiar odor, one that brought back memories of his childhood. When he stepped on a tie, it was so gummy that he changed his gait to walk on the stones instead.

He felt a lump in his throat. His lips started to quiver, and he began to weep. He wept for his miserable childhood and the devastating pain his mother endured at the hands of his Uncle Billy. The poor woman! He recalled the many visitors that used to frequent his home. His mother had a busy schedule. Male callers inundated the premises on a daily basis. Uncle Billy made sure she was busy. And the time he beat her with a belt… if I had a gun, I would have killed him. That bastard!

It wasn't until I was older that I realized what was going on… the drugs, the sex and everything. In fact, I didn't fully understand the extent of it until I moved in with Wayne and Molly.

But everyone knew she was my mother, and everyone knew she was the town whore. Boy, did she ever humiliate me at school! I would never ask a girl out on a date. I was too embarrassed to have any friends. Why did she do this to me? Why did she make my life so miserable? Why didn't she have Billy put in jail or at least have the police stop him from abusing her? He wiped away his tears with his shirt sleeves. I guess the only way to get things done in this town is to do it yourself. Vigilante justice! Yes! That's the best way to operate around here! I still might kill Billy!

Tyler walked past the tall grass, the area Lefty's deputies supposedly searched. He stopped walking when he twisted his ankle on something wedged between the stones. He looked down and saw a rectangular object about one inch wide and three inches long. While it was clearly decimated by train wheels, it had the pattern and texture of a deer's antler.

My dad and I used to make knife handgrips out of deer antlers up in Schroon Lake, he thought to himself. He has a whole collection of stag handled Bowie knives. He looked closer. There was a fragment of a cross guard at the base – designed to protect the user's hands. A slight curvature of the object near the top and a deep hole near the base where a blade would have been inserted, convinced Tyler he was looking at the remnants of a large knife – perhaps even a Bowie knife!

This is the handle of the knife that killed my mom! I'm sure of it!

When Tyler arrived home, Molly and Wayne were just sitting down for dinner wondering if Tyler would join them.

"Care to join us, Ty?" Wayne asked.

"No thank you. I am not very hungry." Wayne could tell Tyler was clearly distraught.

"Are you okay?" Molly probed. "You look upset."

"I am definitely not okay! It was my father! I know that for sure now! My father murdered my mother!"

"Tyler, honey, your father hasn't been around here for months!" Molly noted. "How did you arrive at such a conclusion?"

Tyler shared his experience on the railroad tracks and showed them the object he discovered.

"This was the murder weapon!" he declared. "I know that for sure!"

Molly and Wayne looked at the object totally befuddled. "Maybe you should tell us a little more," Wayne said.

Tyler explained why he believed it was the handle to a knife used as the murder weapon and why he was convinced his dad was the guilty party.

"My dad and me…we used to make these antler handgrips up in Schroon Lake all the time. We'd attach the blades and they became the perfect Bowie Knife!"

"Let's take it to the police station and see if they can extract any prints," Wayne said.

"No!" Tyler exclaimed. "Absolutely not!"

Wayne was alarmed by Tyler's unexpected vehemence.

"What's wrong, Tyler?" he asked.

"What do you think is wrong, Wayne?" Molly's voice rose few octaves. "He doesn't want his father to go to jail! That's what's wrong!"

"But Tyler," Wayne continued. "Maybe it will be someone else's prints…someone who is still at large…putting all of us in danger… including you!"

Tyler immediately broke down and began crying hysterically. Molly placed her arms around him, but he was inconsolable. He broke from her embrace, ran up the stairs to his room slamming the door behind him.

"I am so sick and tired of all this shit!" he shouted. He threw himself on his bed and continued crying. "I just can't take it anymore!"

Wayne and Molly stood motionless at the bottom of the stairs. They looked at each other awkwardly and were unsure of what to do next.

"We shouldn't be surprised," Molly said. "We should have seen this coming and been more prepared. Tyler has simply reached his emotional limit."

"Should I go up and talk to him?" Wayne asked.

"I think he needs to be alone for a while, Wayne. Let's just give him some time. The whole thing is just beginning to sink in. I'm sure there's also a lot of anxiety over his father's whereabouts. Tyler idolizes him, and he has been AWOL for months. That's shameful!"

"I wonder if Tyler will want to stay with us?" Wayne queried. "We have to realize this whole thing has been taking a huge toll on you and me as well."

"Wayne, I have grown to love Tyler like he's is my own flesh and blood. With all the disturbing events he's experienced, I feel we have become much closer. But we must keep on communicating with him. We need to stay as close as possible. This is a very vulnerable time in his life. He could go either way."

With that, Wayne walked up to stairs to Tyler's bedroom. He knocked softly on the door.

"Go away! I just need to be alone," came an almost inaudible response from Tyler.

Wayne knocked again. "Can we talk?"

The door appeared to open almost by itself. "I'm in no mood!" Tyler said with his head down. His languid appearance belied a deep inner hostility that was starting to simmer like never before.

Just how much more can this kid take? Wayne wondered.

Tyler sat on the edge of his bed with his legs together. Tears filled his eyes and streamed down his cheeks like small streams. His body was hunched forward receptively. He was ready for Wayne to give him an answer – any answer that exonerated his father from such a heinous act. How could his father murder his mother?

"How well do you know your father?"

"We've spent lots of time together hunting and fishing in the mountains."

"So, you know him pretty well then, huh?"

"Yeah, we used to have many honest discussions, especially in the evenings around the campfire. Even though, sometimes he didn't act it, I knew he loved my mom very much. He told me he did. He used to apologize for not being home. He used the word 'wanderlust' a lot."

"In the book we read in school entitled Travels with a Donkey, by Robert Louis Stevenson. The author said:

'I travel not to go anywhere, but to go. I travel for travel's sake.'"

"Same with my dad. He didn't need to go anywhere, he just couldn't stay in one spot very long."

"Did you love him any less for that?" Wayne asked.

"Yeah, when I was younger, I did. I used to get mad when he came home for a day or so then left. It wasn't very considerate to my mom either, especially when Uncle Billy moved in."

"What do you think, Ty? In your heart of hearts do you really think your dad would murder your mother?"

Tyler didn't take long.

"No way!" he said vehemently. "No way!"

"Then, if you feel that strongly, we shouldn't have to worry about your dad's prints being on the knife handle, should we?"

"No, I guess not."

CHAPTER TWENTY-SIX

October – 1995–Bridgetown

When Heather Newman, Lefty's clerk, arrived for work at 10:30 a.m., Igor Gunderson was just walking out.

"And who might you be?" he asked

Heather froze.

"What's the problem, bitch? You can't answer a simple question?"

"Her name is Heather. She's my helper. Leave her alone."

Igor looked at Lefty with a hatred in his eyes. "She's mine now!"

"Heather, this is Igor Gunderson. Just do what he says."

"I'm the new deputy in charge around here," Igor declared. "You work for me now! Here is my first order: Find Thomas Prescott and tell him to meet me at the Hampton Inn tonight at 8:00 p.m. sharp. He's gonna work for me too! Do you understand that?"

"Yes, Sir, 8:00 p.m. sharp!" Heather restated his words quickly as if he held the key to her continued existence – and—he probably did.

After Igor departed, Lefty strolled back into his office to lick his wounds. I've never been more insulted in my life, he said to himself. I need to speak to someone. I need some advice.

As unusual as it was for Lefty to seek counsel, his predicament demonstrated just how desperate he was. He felt fear and resentment but more than anything else he felt dishonored and disrespected, two very sobering emotions for a person with the magnitude of Lefty's ego.

"Heather, I'm going to see if I can find Michael – if he's back from the Adirondacks yet."

"I saw Jeff when I stopped for gas at the mobile mart this morning. He was headed to the North Side."

"Well, halleluiah! The mountain boy returns! Probably picking up lottery tickets and a twelve pack–he's getting started early. Michael must be back too."

"That new strip joint called Cheetahs just opened. I think the whole town is there for an early lunch."

"Lunch, my ass!" Lefty shrugged his shoulders in disbelief. "Seeing bouncing boobs is more like it!"

"Lefty, you know the word around town is that Megan kicked Michael out of the house because he was messing around with Francine."

"Of all people…Michael Alexander. The model citizen. Whoever would have thought that of him…having an affair with his best friend's wife. Well, I guess it can happen to the best of them. Maybe someday it will happen to me…if I get lucky."

"You should try Cheetahs. Maybe you'll catch them both there."

"Good idea, Heather."

When Lefty entered Cheetahs, loud strip joint music was playing on a juke. Two girls on an oval stage were pole dancing. He went to the rear of the restaurant where he found Jeff and Michael in a booth having an early lunch.

"You guys look like you were riding hard and were put away wet. Rough trip, huh?"

"Yes, it was, Lefty." Michael answered but was unwilling to elaborate.

"Well at least the wolves didn't get you," Lefty joked.

Michael nearly choked on his Martini. Jeff started to laugh, "There ain't no wolves up there, Lefty! There are more wolves right here in Bridgetown!"

"May I join you dudes?" he asked.

"Sure. What the hell," Jeff replied. "You ain't gonna arrest me, are you?"

"Listen, Festus. Right now, I got much bigger fish to fry than you!"

"Why? What's going on?" Michael casually asked.

"Well… let me tell you boys something; a grizzly bear the size of a boxcar walked into Luigi's this morning. Then he came over to the jail. He introduced himself as Igor Gunderson, Francine's father."

"Holy shit!" Jeff shrieked nearly choking on his French fries.

"He said he wanted to 'waste' both of you." Lefty said with a smug self-righteous smile.

"He said 'waste'?" Michael asked.

"Yeah man! 'waste'! Now exactly what would you like me to do about it?"

Michael became furious. He looked over at Jeff and then at Lefty, leaned back in the booth and said, "Lefty…let me ask you…what the hell do you think you should do about it? Some guy comes into town and threatens to kill two people and the chief of police has to ask the potential victims what he should do about it? Give me a break! Do you know what the word abdicate means?"

"It means being a wuss!" Jeff interjected. "It means Lefty is going to sit on his ass and do nothing because he is scared shitless of this guy."

"Well, that's just great!" Michael said. Just when I thought I needed to dedicate my time and efforts to mend fences with Megan, now I have to worry about defending myself from some lunatic redneck from West Virginia.

"Michael, the guy thinks we killed his daughter." Jeff said.

"Francine?" Michael remembered Francine telling him about her father.

"Well, who do you think, you rockhead?" Lefty added.

Michael was getting more pissed off at Lefty by the second.

"Look! Cut the crap, Lefty! Give a straight answer!" Michael said.

"Michael! Forget it!" Jeff declared, "He ain't capable of a straight answer. Here's the story…I was seeing Francine when I worked at the coal mine in West Virginia. This guy Igor – he was the fire boss and just happened to be Francine's old man. Nobody and I mean nobody messed with this dude. He probably wants to take both our asses back to the coal mine and ring our bodies through the coal cutting machine."

"Goddamn it, Jeff!"

"I'm really sorry, Michael. I can tell you one thing for sure. This guy has taken several people to the coal cruncher and the other miners–they wouldn't dare squeal on him."

"So, what do you intend to do about it, Lefty"?

"Well, for starters…I deputized him," Lefty said. "My best deputy, Thomas Prescott is going to help him."

"You did what!" Jeff shouted.

"No way!" Michael said. "Even someone as stupid as you wouldn't have done that!"

"Michael, don't you see?" Jeff observed. "It takes him completely off the hook! And once the news gets out that we have been arrested for Francine's murder, Lefty's stock goes way up in town and he'll get himself re-elected!"

"Yeah, I may even run for Mayor," Lefty said with arrogant smirk.

"Clever, Lefty. Very clever Lefty!" Michael said caustically.

"Anyway, it's about goddamn time you two jokers got your comeuppance! Have a nice day!"

"So, is that what you came here to tell us?" Michael asked.

"Actually, I came here for advice. But you boys helped me figure out exactly what I am going to do."

With that, Lefty got up, ambled to the bar, plunked his big butt on a stool, and watched the rest of the show.

After lunch, Michael drove to Wayne and Molly's house. He felt compelled to solicit Wayne and Molly's advice on the recent turn of events regarding Igor "The Enforcer" and also wanted to discuss the state of affairs in the Bridgetown Police Department.

When Michael explained their encounter with Lefty at Cheetahs bar, Wayne and Molly were only mildly surprised.

"They're a bunch of derelicts at that police department!" Molly said. "I've never seen anything like it! My experience with them when

Tyler was lost was just awful – certainly enough to convince me we need a new police chief and deputies. I'm still trying to figure out what happened to me up in the sand pits. You know what? I wouldn't trust that Thomas Prescott as far as I could throw him. And I wouldn't be surprised if he was the one who hit me. Good thing Tyler came along when he did!"

"Then there was that other incident up there with those two college kids," Wayne chimed in. "There was no further mention of it, no prints, no investigation, no nothing!"

"We have a major crisis of competency in the police department," Michael concluded. "And something needs to be done about it before innocent people get hurt. The question is: What are we going to do about it?"

"Or the question is: What exactly are we able to do about it? None of our rights have been violated," Molly correctly observed.

"Not yet," Michael noted with a half-smile. "But once I'm dead, it will be impossible to do anything about it."

"Does anyone know anything about this guy Thomas Prescott?" Wayne asked.

"Well, I can tell you this much," Michael said. "Lefty deputized Igor and now Prescott reports to him."

"This guy Igor – nobody even knows him! And, he's a deputy? You got to be kidding!" Wayne frowned with disgust. "How can he get away with that?"

"He's the Chief of Police! He can deputize Dracula if he wants to," Michael calmly observed.

Wayne reached into his pocket and pulled out the knife handle.

"Tyler found it on the railroad tracks yesterday across from his former home. We both think it is a knife handle and could very well be the murder weapon."

"I took this over to Lt. James Williams, the county undersheriff. He is in charge of the county forensic lab and has spoken several times to my classes about the science of forensics."

"I know him too," Michael said. "He comes into Luigi's for breakfast a few days a week. Good guy."

"Yeah, well, as a special favor, I asked him to check the item for prints. He said to call him this afternoon."

Wayne excused himself and went into the kitchen to make the call. When he returned, a look of startled disbelief blanketed his face.

"Oh my God! You won't believe it! It's Dr. Kazuya's prints!" he said. "He's Tyler's counselor at school…the guy Tyler believes has helped him deal with the bullying issue."

"Unbelievable! Of all people!" Molly said.

Wayne walked over to the living room window and said, "Tyler shared with me a conversation he had at lunch with Dr. Kazuya. Apparently, during the war his mother was forced into sexual slavery by the Japanese military after his father was executed. He was only ten years old at the time when his mother was gang raped right in front of him. Can you imagine the trauma he must have felt? He told Tyler he turned into a vicious animal. He wanted to kill them all!'"

"He said she was bleeding all over and was in extreme shock and that he couldn't bear to see her suffer. He said Dr. Kazuya gently placed the blanket over her face until she stopped breathing altogether."

"He killed her!" Molly said. "There is no two ways about it! He killed her!"

"No, Molly. That's how I saw it too. He said Dr. Kazuya just helped her to… stop breathing… as if it was some sort of mercy killing."

"This guy is some sort of sicko and Tyler has an appointment with him later in the afternoon," Molly noted.

"Molly, do you think Tyler is safe?" Michael asked.

"I'll tell you this; I don't like the idea of him being alone with Dr. Kazuya, that's for sure!"

"Okay, then," Michael said. "Wayne and Molly…you go to the school and see if you can find Tyler. I'll see if I can find Jeff and that Igor character before he does some irreparable damage. He needs to know that Jeff and I did not kill his daughter!"

Chapter Twenty-Seven

September – 1995–Bridgetown

Tyler Walden arrived on time for his afternoon appointment with Dr. Kazuya. The combined weight of running away from home and his mother's murder created a heavy burden for the young man to carry. Finding what he thought to be the murder weapon on the railroad tracks only added to his nervousness.

"I'm so sorry to hear about your Mom, Tyler. How are you feeling right now?"

"Oh, I don't know," Tyler replied despondently. "Sad, I guess."

"Lonesome too I'll bet." Dr. Kazuya added.

"Yeah, I guess so. More than anything else, I'm scared. Who knows where my dad is. I thought he cared about me, but I haven't seen him in months. My mom…she was trying so hard to get better. I even hoped the day might come…" Tyler broke down and began to sob. "My life has been like a football where everyone just keeps handing me off to someone else."

Dr. Kazuya put his head in his hands. He dropped them quickly as if he was revealing something about himself he wasn't supposed to show.

"You said 'the day might come'. Would you please finish that?"

"When we all would be together as one family again. That's impossible to happen now. Who, knows. Maybe it always was impossible, and I just didn't want to believe it."

"So, tell me Tyler, why are you scared?"

"This town is a very dangerous place to live, Dr. Kazuya. First my dad leaves me, then my Uncle Billy moves in and beats up my mom and me. Then he turns her into a prostitute. Next thing I know someone kills my mom and attacks my foster mom! I'm probably next in line! I'm getting the hell out of this place just as soon as I can! And I'm moving far, far away!"

"Your wounds are deep, aren't they, Ty?"

"Yeah, they sure are. Sometimes I feel so angry, I want to punch someone! At school I am always embarrassed by the bullies. Wayne is right there and sees everything. I always let him down. I hate myself for that."

"Too bad some people can't get their acts together, isn't it?"

"What about Wayne and Molly. Do you think they care?"

"Sure, they care but they are not my real mom and dad."

"Do you love them?"

"I don't even know what love is."

Dr. Kazuya leaned back in his chair placing his right hand on his forehead and began rubbing it vigorously. He inhaled deeply then exhaled to release the tension of the moment. Then he leaned forward and said, "Do you feel you need to be someone else when you are around them?"

"Yeah, sometimes I do. I feel I owe them so much I would never want to disappoint them. I guess that's why I ran away after I dropped the pass in the end zone."

"I think you are old enough to understand this now. Even if you're not, I'm still going to take the risk of telling you anyway. Kids who live with repeated abandonment experiences often end up feeling shame. Shame arises from the painful message implied in abandonment: 'You are not important. You are not of value.' This is real pain that if left unaddressed can cause a lot of emotional damage later in life."

Tyler got up from the chair and walked around Dr. Kazuya's office. With his outstretched arms, he leaned over the front of the desk trying to hold back his tears.

He looked over to Dr. Kazuya and asked. "So, how should I deal with it?"

"It will take courage and determination on your part Tyler. You decide…who you want to live with…Wayne and Molly or your dad? I want you to think on that question for a few days."

"I have already decided. I want to be with Wayne and Molly. Actually, Dr. Kazuya, I have no choice. My father doesn't stay in one place long enough to be good father. He'd rather live in the woods than in a house like normal people."

"I think that's a good choice, though."

"Probably is since my father is nowhere around." Tyler stood up to leave.

"Oh, by the way, could I give you a lift home? I'm leaving now too."

"Sure. If it's not too much trouble."

"None whatsoever."

As they left Dr. Kazuya's office, Tyler encountered Brad Kutcher in the hallway, one of the formidable linemen on the football team. Brad couldn't resist intimidating Tyler any chance he could.

"Hey Bucko, he said. "Too bad you came back to school. I mean after dropping that pass we were hoping you'd never come back!"

Tyler stopped and looked at Brad with a frightening stare. Then he fearlessly walked up to Brad, wound up and punched him in the face so hard he went down for the count.

"From now on," Tyler said, "when you open your mouth to mock me, I'm going to close it for you."

Tyler walked past several members of the football team. They gave him a wide berth and some even gave him a thumbs up sign. A few patted him on the back and said, "Nice punch, Ty!"

Dr. Kazuya stood motionless – amazed at Tyler's new-found audacity. "Feel better now?" he asked.

"Not really," Tyler replied.

Dr. Kazuya's 1986 Toyota Corolla was almost silent as he drove it slowly as if he were in a parade. Tyler wondered why he just didn't step on the gas and get on with it. While his eyes were riveted on the road, his quietness instilled an eerie sensation in Tyler.

"You missed the turn, Dr. Kazuya."

"Yes, I know, Tyler. I want to show you something."

Dr. Kazuya drove to the outskirts of town toward the Romano Sand Pits.

"Why are we going up there?"

"Be patient, Tyler. Just trust me."

"I do trust you, Dr. Kazuya. More than anyone."

But Tyler was still puzzled. Why the heck was Dr. Kazuya taking me up to the sand pits? Still, having always trusted Dr. Kazuya, he was afraid he might spoil the friendship by showing any signs of fear.

When they arrived at the entrance of the sand pits, Dr. Kazuya drove around the barricades then proceeded up the hill into a wooded area where wild brush and tall trees slowed their forward progress.

After they passed the workers and their earthmoving vehicles on a nearby hill, they drove to the farthest point of the sand pits – a place where no one ever went. They approached a large mound of dirt. A pick and shovel rested conspicuously at the bottom of the mound.

"We have arrived," Dr. Kazuya announced as if he was a tour guide. "This is where I've spent my weekends for the last five years."

Now Tyler was really confused. Did he bring me all the way up here to show me a mound of dirt?

"This area was dug out several years ago by an old steam shovel. It lifted out most of the rocks and soil and dumped everything over there," Dr. Kazuya explained pointing to the mound of dirt on the left side of the trench and a small mountain of rock on the other side.

"I've been working on this project every chance I get."

"Is it some kind of cave?" Tyler asked.

"I guess you could call it cave, especially the front area, but I've also dug a couple of tunnels that are quite long."

"So, this is what you do with your free time?"

"My ancestors used the solitude of caves to meditate and the tunnels to escape from the enemy."

"But, Dr. Kazuya…you don't have any enemies."

"Sometimes you don't know who your real enemies are."

"Where are we going?"

"Follow me," he said. They walked down a sloping path to a facade of broken tree limbs and uprooted bushes that were piled on top of a small iron gate in front of a three-foot tunnel entrance.

"I realize I must do a better job of camouflaging this entrance," Dr. Kazuya said matter-of-factly as he removed the brush and unlocked the padlock on the gate.

He began to walk through the open gate into the narrow entrance way.

"C'mon, Tyler. Don't be afraid."

A small knapsack was just inside the gate. Dr. Kazuya took off his shirt, tie, and trousers neatly folding them and placing them on a small wooden picnic table. He unzipped the knapsack and removed a pair of white cotton pants, t-shirt, and headband.

"What are you doing?" Tyler asked curiously.

"Oh, I never work up here without showing honor. Life is all about honor."

"This is the Japanese Hachimaki (head band) that belonged to my father." 慈恵 was written in bright red letters on the front of it.

"What does that mean?"

"Its Japanese for 'mercy and love'. Originally–and still today – Hachimakis' are worn at festivals to ward off evil spirits. During the war they were supposed to instill courage and honor and ward off the enemy."

"And on my t-shirt… Anrakushi, literally means 'peaceful and honorable death'."

"Tyler, my religion is based on veneration of ancestors who get very angry if a descendant lowers the reputation of the family name. I come from a culture that believes any person who dishonors family… who creates shame for their family… needs to die. In fact, death is the only way to restore the family honor."

Tyler was feeling uneasy. He didn't quite understand what Dr. Kazuya was trying to say.

"I've watched you suffer, Tyler. I have watched as your friends have berated and humiliated you and your family. I would go home and cry for you after our meetings. No young man your age should have to endure such dishonor. Your mother cast shame on you and she deserved to die."

Tyler stiffened up. He gasped with fear and needed to catch his breath before he could respond.

"You killed my mom, didn't you?"

With his arms rigid by his side, Dr. Kazuya bowed respectfully.

"I did it for you and your father. Now you can regain your family honor."

"You killed her! You killed her!" Tyler screamed.

"No, Tyler, I just helped her to… stop breathing."

Tyler turned and ran out of the cave as fast as he could. He didn't stop running until he arrived at the high school parking lot, a few miles away.

Wayne and Molly were just driving out of the parking lot having searched the school for signs of Tyler and Dr. Kazuya.

"I figured he would have gone to my office after his appointment with Kazuya. Lately, he has wanted to ride home with me after school."

"Let's drive by the house and see if he's there." Molly said.

As they drove out of the parking lot, they became alarmed when he saw Tyler hunched over on one knee on the side of the road. He was out of breath and shaking as if he had seen the devil.

"Tyler! Are you okay?" Wayne shouted through the open window. "Get in the car!"

"No! I'm not okay!" he said as he opened the car door and tumbled onto the back seat allowing gravity to do all the work. Tyler's head dropped forward, and he closed his eyes. He appeared weak and lightheaded. His breathing was rapid yet shallow. Then he fell sideways and lost consciousness.

Wayne got out of the car to attend to Tyler. "Tyler! Tyler!" Wayne shook him gently, but Tyler was unconscious.

"Oh my God. Is he going to be alright?" Molly stammered.

Wayne recognized the symptoms. "Tyler has gone into shock," he said. He checked and detected a pulse then he noticed Tyler was still breathing.

"We need to get him to the hospital fast!" Wayne exclaimed. Highland Hospital was not far from the high school.

After the hospital doctors worked on Tyler for a few minutes, he regained some consciousness, yet was very lethargic and disoriented.

"I have no idea where to find Jeff," Wayne said to Molly

"Nor do I, Honey, but we can worry about finding Jeff later," Molly said.

A doctor came over to where they were seated.

"Tyler must have suffered some kind of traumatic event," he said. "I think we should keep an eye on him and when he wakes up, he'll tell us what happened to him."

"Well, if you ask me, it has something to do with his appointment with Dr. Kazuya," Molly said. "He just saw him this afternoon! That creep!"

"Can we see him now?" Wayne asked.

"Yes. We can see if he is awake yet," the doctor said.

When they arrived in Tyler's room, Tyler sat up and hugged them both.

"I love you both!" he said.

"Honey, what happened to you?" Molly asked.

"Dr. Kazuya! He did it! He killed my mom!" Tyler cried.

"He's up in the pits – in a cave – performing some kind of Japanese ritual. Hurry–call the police! Call the police!"

"Okay. Okay, Ty. Calm down," Wayne said. "We know. The prints on the knife handle were his. We've already informed the authorities. I'll call now and tell them where he is."

"Rest for now, Honey," Molly said warmly. We will let you know what happens with Dr. Kazuya." Tyler eye lids were heavy as he placed his head back on the pillow. Within five minutes, he was fast asleep.

CHAPTER TWENTY-EIGHT

September – 1995 – Jeff's Parents' House

Meanwhile, unaware of Tyler's situation or that Dr. Kazuya was the one who murdered his wife, Jeff had one singular focus: find Igor and kill him!

"I'm here just for a little while, Ma, okay?"

"Jeffrey, I tell you and your brother all the time – this is still your home and you are always welcome here."

"Thanks, Ma."

Jeff located his .12-gauge double barreled shotgun in the garage, the one he used to shoot geese and ducks in his Schroon Lake blind. Jeff sawed the barrel when he was a teenager. It had two triggers, one for each barrel. If by accident, both barrels were pulled simultaneously, the recoil could break a person's clavicle.

With Igor's belligerent non-negotiable attitude and Lefty's apparent capitulation, Jeff realized the possibility of Michael and his survival would depend entirely on going after Igor himself; not sitting back and waiting for Igor to find him. Jeff knew he had to be the aggressor.

If I shoot the bastard, I'll be arrested for murder and then they'll indict me for Francine's murder too. One thing is for sure, that fat ass ain't never gonna get me back to Morgantown and use the chili-dog machine on me! And, not only that – I ain't gonna sit around and wait for him to find me. I'm going after him! All I gotta do is find his big black Hummer parked in front of some motel. Then he's dead meat. I'll ship his fat carcass back to Morgantown in a black box!

"Ma. Could I borrow your car for a while? I have some errands to run."

"Be back for dinner at 6:00 p.m. and tell that brother of yours it's been a year now since we've seen him. Your father's eighty-fifth birthday is Sunday. I'd like both of you boys to show up. You know he isn't well, and this could be his last birthday."

"Ma! I have no idea where the hell Billy is. Our paths never cross."

"Jeffrey! Goddamn it! He is your brother! Find him!"

"Okay, okay, Ma. I'll try."

Jeff packed the .12-gauge shotgun in the trunk of the car. He included a box of Winchester heavy shot charge .12-gauge shotgun ammo. He donned his Safe Life bullet proof vest, then pulled out of the garage and went looking for his prey. "I'm probably going to end up in the slammer the rest of my life, but this guy will kill me, and Michael and I also want to protect my son, Tyler from this monster. This is the only solution!

CHAPTER TWENTY-NINE

September – 1995 – Hampton Inn

Igor Gunderson drove his large, attention getting black Hummer to the Hampton Inn on the outskirts of town. After checking in, he parked in the front of the hotel, in the most prominent location he could find so that the rear bumper sticker that said–skull and crossbones–coal miner with an attitude was visible from the road.

Michael was driving around town aimlessly looking for Igor's Hummer. But he simply could not concentrate. This is just too unbelievable to be happening, he said to himself.

With all that has transpired during the last few days, the stark realities of the damage I have done to my own family are starting to sink in. I want to reconcile with Megan more than ever, but I just don't think she would be very receptive. Where is my life headed? he kept asking himself. He began to cry uncontrollably and needed to pull over to the side of the road.

I'll do anything to get Megan to forgive me. I'm going to get down on my knees and beg for her forgiveness. I can't live without her and my boys. I also have to resurrect my financial planning practice. I hate to think how many clients I've lost over this Francine thing.

Finally, as dusk set in, he drove to the Hampton Inn to spend the night. When he arrived, he saw Igor's Hummer parked under the lights. He noticed the West Virginia license plates and the bumper sticker and concluded that it must belong to that guy Igor Gunderson, the coal miner and fire boss from West Virginia, the new deputy, as Lefty called him.

When Michael approached the office to check in, he said to the Innkeeper, "There's a rather big guy who just recently took a room. His name is Igor Gunderson. Could you give me his room number please?"

"Sure. But I wouldn't mess with that dude," the Innkeeper said. "He is bigger than a house and looks meaner than an ally cat."

"I just need to let him know we found his daughter's killer."

"Well, I hope that person is behind bars. Otherwise, this guy will tear his limbs off. At any rate, he is in room 42. Its right around the corner. Good luck!"

Michael thought about it for a minute. Do I really need backup? All this guy wants is to know is who murdered his daughter. Now we know it was Dr. Kazuya. Once he understands that neither Jeff nor I committed the murder, we'll be off the hook.

Michael knocked on the door of room 42. He waited a few minutes then knocked again. The door opened abruptly slamming back against the wall.

An enormous hulk of a man standing doorway with a bottle of beer in his hand angrily asked, "Who the hell are you and what the fuck do you want?"

Michael trembled for a moment but then recovered. "My name is Michael Alexander and..." Before Michael could explain himself, Igor grabbed him by the throat and threw him on the floor of the motel room.

"You killed my daughter and you have the balls to come to my room?"

"Allow me to explain. We found…." Michael couldn't finish. Igor kicked him in the stomach twice with his heavy steel toed muck boots. As Michael was doubled over and writhing in pain on the floor, Igor slowly and deliberately placed a set of oversized brass knuckles on his right fist making sure they on tight. I love the feel of bones crushing, he said to himself. Then he picked Michael up by the collar with his left hand and punched him hard three times in the face. Bleeding profusely, Michael slumped helplessly to the floor unconscious.

Igor stepped outside to survey the premises. Just then Thomas Prescott showed up in a police cruiser.

"And…you must be my new deputy Thomas Prescott," he said.

Looking at Michael unconscious on the floor, Thomas said, "My God! We have to get this guy to the hospital or he is going to bleed to death right in front of us."

"Don't you even think of moving him!" Igor asserted.

"What the hell are you talking about. This man is going to die!" Thomas bent down and began to move Michael toward his police car.

Angered by Thomas's defiance, Igor cracked him hard on his head with his right fist, the one with the brass knuckles.

"I warned you!" he said. "Now I have two lads for the chili-dog machine!"

As Thomas and Michael lay unconscious, Jeff spotted the Hummer from the highway.

"Okay…now I've got that fat bastard!" he said as he pulled in and parked right behind Thomas's police cruiser. He opened the trunk and secured his .12-gauge double-barreled shot gun checking to make sure it was loaded. He walked confidently up to the motel room door. He had a job to do and knew this was the only answer. He knocked hard then stood back about ten feet. As soon as Igor answered and was visible in the doorway, Jeff pulled both triggers on the shotgun and blew Igor's head clean off. As the kickback from the shotgun drove Jeff back and knocked him off of his feet. He clutched his shoulder, closed his eyes, and stiffened up with pain.

Once Jeff got back on his feet, he ran into the hotel room. Kneeling next to Michael, he was stunned by his bloodied, disfigured appearance and could barely believe it was really Michael lying there.

"My God, Michael, what did that bastard do to you?" Deeply upset, he still somehow managed to call 911.

Within fifteen minutes, two ambulances arrived. The paramedics quickly assessed the situation then immobilized Michael and Thomas with backboards in preparation for the trip to the hospital.

Jeff approached one paramedic who was monitoring Michael's vital signs. When he asked how Michael was doing, he shook his head slowly and said, "Not good."

"Can I ride along?"

"Sorry Pal. Not a good idea. He's unconscious and seriously injured and we have to keep close tabs on him. You can meet us at Moses Ludington Hospital in Ticonderoga.

"Moses Ludington?" Jeff reiterated.

"It's the best trauma hospital in the area."

"Yes, I know from my own first-hand experience. This really is déjà vu all over again, he said to himself.

Jeff was disconsolate when he arrived at Moses Ludington Hospital. He felt an overpowering sadness and with every step fought tearing up, but his willpower was gone, shattered by recent events. He began to weep. Locating the nearest lavatory, he found an empty stall, covered his face with tissue and wept harder than he had ever wept before. No matter how hard he tried, he couldn't stop. This time, his best friend, Michael was the injured one and he was the advocate.

When Jeff found Michael's hospital room, Dr. Rheingold was hovering over him with anguish written on his face.

"Mr. Walden…you caused quite a commotion around here when you left so abruptly. But I'm glad you survived your injuries. I don't think your friend will be as lucky."

"Can I speak with him?" Jeff said still struggling not to break down.

"He must have been hit in the face by a bulldozer. Most of the bones in his face are broken and he has a fractured skull. He is in and out of consciousness. I'll try to get his attention." He gently shook Michael's arm.

"Someone is here to see you Mr. Alexander."

Michael opened his eyes. "Jeff?" he whispered.

"Yes, it's me, Michael."

"Seems like we got this situation reversed," Michael murmured. "You're the one that's supposed to be in the hospital bed and I'm supposed to be standing over you."

"Not this time, Michael. Igor cracked you pretty good."

"Did you get him?"

"Yeah, blew his goddamn head off! Blew it all the way back to Morgantown!"

"Jeff, you are my best friend. You know that, right?"

"Yes, for sure and I'm very lucky for that. Hang in there buddy. Dr. Rheingold is right here."

"Never mind the doctor. Where is the Snork! How the hell else am I going to get out of here? He smiled but Jeff could see he was in great pain.

"Why? You're not thinking of escaping, are you? Want to try another pillow in the blanket trick?" Jeff smiled. The comic relief felt good.

"You son-of-a-bitch…what you put me through."

"I can't believe you never found me," Jeff said softly.

"Jeff will you please do me two favors?"

"Sure. Anything you want Michael. Anything."

"First, promise me that you will become a Forest Ranger. It would be a meaningful way for you to spend the rest of your life. You know how much you love the outdoors. You could settle down and spend more time with Tyler."

Jeff hesitated for a few seconds then said, "Yes, I promise, Michael. The last few months made me realize it's time for me to carve out a new way of life for Tyler and me."

"Good, Jeff. I'm so glad to hear that."

"Secondly, Jeff." Michael began to falter. "Will you please tell Megan and my boys I love them and that I am deeply sorry for what I have done?"

Jeff put his head down. He was already sobbing but didn't want Michael to notice.

"Yes, I will do that for you Michael."

"Thanks, Buddy."

Michael took a deep breath. Jeff gripped his hand tightly. Then Michael exhaled, turned his head, and passed away.

CHAPTER THIRTY

September – 1995 – Romano Sand Pits – Bridgetown

Chief Lefty Margolis leaned back in his plush executive chair, placed his heavy engineer boots on the corner of the desk, took a sip of Jim Beam, and breathed a big sigh of relief. While Thomas Prescott was still in the hospital with injuries inflicted by Igor, he was expected to recover and return to his job.

But there were several other events that were worthy of celebration: Igor was dead. Lefty didn't have to be insulted by him anymore. Michael was dead. Lefty no longer had to deal with his pestering. And, finally, Francine's killer was identified. Lefty was beginning to feel like the hero he always thought he was.

The only problem was that Dr. Kazuya was still at large. Lefty sent Ralph Williams, his other deputy, up to the Romano Sand Pits to find and arrest Dr. Kazuya. But Ralph did neither.

"He must have disappeared into the cave tunnels," Ralph tried hard to explain but Lefty was unreceptive.

"Well, why didn't you go the hell in there after him," Lefty asked with his usual testiness.

"I ain't going in no tunnels for nobody!" Ralph asserted.

"Awe fuck it! I guess I gotta do everything myself around here!" Lefty stood up from his chair and started to walk out of the office.

"Where are you going?" Heather asked.

"I'm gonna take a ride up to the sand pits and see if I can find this Kazuya character."

"Well…okay. Be careful now."

Lefty drove all over the sand pits. He finally went to the far end and located large mounds of dirt and an open cave right next to them.

"Anyone in there," he hollered, bending over and placing his forehead into the cave first.

Suddenly, Lefty felt the debilitating pain of a taser probe on his head totally incapacitating him. He fell head first into the cave opening and lay unconscious in the hard dirt.

Later that day, one of the Romano bulldozers filled the cave with dirt.

No one in Bridgetown has ever heard from Lefty or Dr. Kazuya again. And, no one really gave a tinker's damn either.

CHAPTER THIRTY-ONE

September- 1995 – Highland Hospital – Bridgetown

As Tyler left the hospital with Wayne and Molly, he suddenly stopped dead in his tracks.

"Dad! Dad!" he bellowed. Jeff was leaning up against a bright red Harley Davidson with a smile on his face as wide as the handlebars. Tyler ran full speed almost knocking Jeff and over as he reached him. He embraced his father with a bear hug around his ribs and spine that almost suffocated him.

"I love you so much!" he said.

Big tears streamed down Tyler's face. The sadness he endured with Dr. Kazuya combined with the elation of seeing his father for the first time in several months was overwhelming.

"Whoa, Ty! Your old man ain't what he used to be!"

"Dad! I've missed you so much! Where have you been?"

"It's a long story, Ty. When we have a few hours to talk, I'll tell you all about it. But I'm here right now and I plan on being here for a long time."

"Where did you get this unbelievable machine?" Tyler asked as his eyes nearly popped out of his head.

"Do you like it?"

"It's magnificent!"

"Well…its yours! Have to wait a couple years before you can drive it… legally that is! In the meantime, you and me, we'll ride it all over the Adirondacks and fish all the lakes up there! I know this won't make up for all the birthdays and Christmas' I've missed, but in a small way, it is something I can do for you."

"Dad. I don't know what to say." A torrent of tears continued to dribble down Tyler's face as if he couldn't turn the spigot off.

"Just remember…I have always loved you and I always will."

"Thank you so much!"

"Okay…are we ready to roll?"

"You know I am!"

Tyler waved goodbye to Wayne and Molly and Jeff and Tyler took off on the Harley.

"Hang on Ty! This may be a rough ride."

"Hey Dad – don't you know by now? I'm used to rough rides!"

ABOUT THE AUTHOR

Not only is writing a natural outgrowth of Roger's formal education; it is a product of his diverse life experience. The University of Rochester and St. Bonaventure University provided a solid foundation, but like Mark Twain once said, "Never let your book learning interfere with your education."

Teaching high school English for three years and coaching football along with a thirty-year field leadership position with Ameriprise Financial was his "apprenticeship" for writing and provided a very significant "education", especially with regard to human behavior.

See Roger's other books at: **www.rogercorea.com**

9 780578 853338